JOU... THROUGH THE DYING LANDS

A

MÖRK BORG

FICTION ANTHOLOGY

COMPILED BY
JOHN BALTISBERGER

MADNESS HEART GAMES

Madness Heart Press
2006 Idlewilde Run Dr.
Austin, Texas 78744

Cover Art by Simone Tametta

Interior Layout by Lori Michelle
www.TheAuthorsAlley.com

For more information, address:
john@madnessheart.press

www.madnessheart.press

Dedicated to Brian Colin, Christian Eichhorn,
and Philip Reed

CONTENTS

COFFIN BERTH

CHARLES R. BERNARD

IT WAS RÄTROT GILTRETCH'S last handful of silver, and he clutched it with a scrawny, pallid fist that had seen better days.

The hackman watched him unclench his grasp, one pallid finger at a time. He then picked through Rätrot's offering with practiced, black-gloved fingers of his own.

The last scion of the Giltretch Barony (little more this last century than a ruin, shrouded by death, and rumors too unspeakable to be expressed in more than a hushed whisper) knew the hackman only as Reiter. Concluding his appraisal of the silver, Reiter looked at Rätrot with black, beady eyes that glittered through the battered slit of his corroded bascient half helm. His crooked nose held court above a dour, joyless mouth, which now turned down in sour disappointment.

"Is this all?" Reiter asked. His voice was a cold chisel.

Rätrot felt both a burning flood of shame and a freezing blaze of rage. Surely it was enough silver. It *had* to be. Hadn't he traded the last of the Giltretch arms and armor for the gleaming, asymmetrically-struck discs? *Once*, came Rätrot's bitter thought, *the Barony employed a dozen hackmen; ones with proper coaches clad in gilt and glossy crimson paint*. Reiter's hack, by contrast, was a beaten, faded black contraption with a box seat for its mercenary pilot, and not a single berth for passengers. Not those still alive, at any rate.

"That's all I have," said Rätrot. The words were black bile on his tongue.

Reiter's beady orbs took in Rätrot for a moment, weighing him with dispassionate contempt.

Rätrot Giltretch was a thin man, but the driver of the black corpse-wagon could still see the strength left in those ropy limbs. Thin he may have been, but hardly starving. His aristocratic blood was evident from his dress and speech, though Rätrot's condition—his fingers bare of rings, his wardrobe worn nearly threadbare—spoke of a precipitous decline. Reiter's sense of charity, paltry to begin with, shriveled further. A courtier. He *hated* courtiers.

"I risk much," Reiter said, "and in comparison, I ask little. I promise to convey your dead beloved to a proper grave. Which is more dignified than the public pyre, yes? For that simple act, the King would have my head, should I be caught."

It was true. By order of King Fathmu VII, the dead of Schleswig were to be consigned to flame, with no exceptions. A plague had come to Schleswig; a plague both more mysterious and deadlier than prior maladies, many of which had swept in and out of the Wastland like foul breezes from Lake Onda, which lay to the city's east. Those with coin to spend, however, could spare expired loved ones the torch and see them laid to rest with dignity. A few brave, greedy hackmen, Reiter among them, were willing to secret the dead from Schleswig to an ancient, long-forgotten cemetery in the Totholz Forest to the north. Fathmu's soldiers were too diligent to let their guard down to those who might flee, and thus spread the grim affliction running riot in the merchant city. The soldiers only trusted the corpse-bearers to conduct their morbid business and return. The living could do naught for their own souls but grimly wait for the contagion to run its course, damning or sparing them as it saw fit. In death, on the other hand, some dignity could still be saved; one might be laid to rest in the black soil of Totholz, if one's family could scrape together silver for the bribes.

When Reiter balked, Rätrot Giltretch stammered. His composure, never stable, was fractured by this unexpected turn. From his reaction, Reiter saw that this particular stone had been bled dry. To his expert eye, the silver proffered by the little man was genuinely the extent of his remaining wealth.

"Fine enough," the hackman conceded with a sigh. He snatched the coins from Rätrot's pallid palm. "This will buy your father a burial in Stimmen Cemetery, but the coffin's not included." He paused, boring into Rätrot's watery blue eyes. Reiter's vaguely vulpine regard was inscrutable behind the pointed helmet's slit. "And you *need* a coffin. I pilot no meat-barrow of the naked dead."

"Yes. Yes, I understand," the last Giltretch replied, nodding with such fervor that his lank, blonde coiffure came partially unbound and flopped down one cheek like a dead, albino herring.

"Leave his coffin in the alley," Reiter said. "And your man to help me load it. Before first light. I have a narrow window to slip past the city guard's attentions and a narrower one to slip back, even with their palms greased and their blind eye turned."

Rätrot nodded his assent, and thus, the deal was struck.

The next day before dawn, the dead and leaden sky above Schleswig poured its miserly radiance across the city's towers and pavilions like watered milk. It did not bring the light, not yet. It merely bleached away the blackest parts of night. At this hour, many of Schleswig's alleyways and slouching, outer-borough neighborhoods remained steeped in degrees of shadow. Reiter's carriage, the hack which gave the hackman his title and profession, wove nimbly in and out of these penumbrae.

The sable of the horse and buggy were matched by the hackman's tarnished gear. Reiter's face below his bascinet was neutral; the face of one set to perform a day's not-unpleasant work. Now that the dickering was done, he'd shed his scowl. The lone beast hitched to Reiter's carriage was a stringy, slouch-backed mare named Grog. Reiter had already loaded most of his fast-rotting freight by this, the first light of the day, and once the last few coffins had been stowed, he made his way onward without incident.

Passing through the streets of Schleswig, Reiter scrupulously kept his own counsel. While he'd yet to brush King Fathmu's carceral fingertips while slinking out of town against the quarantine and burn orders, respectively, Reiter held firm to caution as a watchword.

Soon, the city's walls were behind him. As the dead sky brightened with the coming dawn, the only sounds which kept the hackman company were the dull and steady tread of Grog's hooves on the thin black soil, and the groaning chorus of creaks and knocks that rose from both the carriage and its carefully-boxed contents.

"Just thee and me, Grog," said Reiter with relief, rolling along the ragged ruts which led to Totholz and its endless, dreaming depths. "Thee, me, and the dead, and that's enough company for my taste."

Grog grunted noncommittally. The malign maw of nature hadn't seen fit to gift her species with a tongue for speech; her sense of smell, however, was outstanding. Good enough to know that Reiter's carriage held a clutch of rotting human corpses . . . and one body, other than that of Reiter himself, which was still very much alive.

No scrivener recorded her last testament, but the first victim of Schleswig's Dancing Plague had most likely come from Schleswig Sanitorium. So historians would later surmise, at any rate. The known facts were far fewer at the time, but this much was certain: on an oddly yellow day, a woman began to dance in Schleswig's market square.

This was no dance of celebration; nor a reel spun out of love of drink. Her eyes, observers would maintain, were wide and lightning-struck with terror. Her limbs jerked and twitched. Her dance was as graceless as a puppet piloted by an untrained, unhinged puppeteer. Her roughspun skirt fanned forth like the blooming of some dun-colored blossom. She danced her uncoordinated reel with a macabre and jolly grin stretched across her frightened and emaciated features.

Novel as the outburst was, a lone lunatic's caper hardly would have warranted much notice. But, before the day had died, she was no longer alone.

It came to be called the Dancing Plague, for staggeringly obvious reasons. Those afflicted would, at first, assume a distracted air. A distant glaze would come over their eyes. Soon the victim would adopt an oddly cocked way of holding their head, as though hearkening to distant, half-heard strains from some phantasmal orchestra.

Finally, the dance. The dance that swept them up completely, legs swinging and heels drumming, until the dancer dropped dead. Interventions were resisted fiercely; restraints were broken by the febrile strength the Dancing Plague lent its rictus-grinning victims.

How this illness spread, none knew with certainty. Some advanced the theorem that a sickening miasma rose from Schleswig's crumbling catacombs and dungeons; others blamed the perilous proximity of the unwholesome waters of Lake Onda. Uncounted years hence, long after Rätrot Giltretch met his unspeakable reckoning, the blame would be laid at the stony, joyless feet of Schleswig Sanitarium. This retroactive blame, of course, did no one in those deathly plague years any good.

The Dancing Plague—known variously as "Parsafal's Polska," "Grolkin's Gambol," or "the Japes"—seized the mercantile city like a debtor's despair. In unnumbered courtyards, squares, and banquet halls, dancers by the dozen formed a whirligig of limbs and bony grins. These flailing figures first grew scrawny, then skeletal, then fell when death at last tapped in. King Fathmu VII watched his city sicken in the grips of an unnatural affliction and acted, sealing Schleswig's borders and closing its unnumbered boneyard to the dead.

"Burn them all," Fathmu decreed.

And of the living?

"Seal the gates," Fathmu said with characteristically grim fatalism. "Some of us shall die. Some shall survive. But whatever our fate, this pernicious plague must not spread further into the Wastland."

Sluggish with despair but stirred to duty, Fathmu's soldiers did as they were bid. Even Schleswig's aristocracy could not escape the city's reckoning; not alive, at least. There were, however, one or two exceptions. In every settlement, whether gilded city or ruined sump, vermin tend to thrive in darkness, death, and dank decay. The same is true of mercenary souls who profit during times of cataclysm, and perhaps no soul in Schleswig was more mercenary than the thin broth of a soul belonging to the hackman named Reiter.

Reiter had survived the Velvet Pox when it held the city of Grift in thrall, and he'd escaped the Blackrot when it sundered what was left of Galgenbeck. Reiter was a hackman, after all; a horse-drawn traveler from land to land and doorstep to doorstep. He'd seen much that left him more inured to plague and misery than most. Physically, as well as morally.

Reiter saw the Dancing Plague as he saw each doom that crossed his glittering gaze; as an opportunity. A deal was struck with the least rigid of King Fathmu's guards, a bargain whereby Reiter was allowed to ferry out the well-heeled dead of Schleswig to a remote burial site—for a fee. Reiter was known to these guards, who thought (correctly) that he feared plague less than he feared a dry throat. He was certain to return to Schleswig, the lone beacon of taverns in a vast, dry sea. The wealthy families of Schleswig, in turn, were more than happy to part with their silver in exchange for a proper interment. They had seen the public pyres, and even in the snug security of their manses, they could taste the ash of the city's disaster, a final judgement in which pauper ash mixed freely with the cinders of noble blood. Reiter's quiet business thrived throughout the plague's jittery-limbed duration.

Reiter considered himself clever; a survivor. Definitionally speaking, he was. "Survivors," he would say, "are simply those who can survive." He'd often frame this costume jewel of wisdom with a long pull on his briar pipe, invariably wreathing his face with clouds of smoke that rose like wise and ghostly eyebrows.

Had Rätrot Giltretch heard this glass pearl fall from the hackman's lips, he would have heartily agreed. In its own crumbling way, the Giltretch clan had lived on, where many once-high, now-fallen families would have fragmented and faded from the barren stones of history. True, what had once been a substantial barony had fallen into bleak decline, brick by rotting brick and one festering, benighted parcel of land at a time. True, the family's wealth had been denuded by successive generations of carrion-feeders, of whose less-than-proud descendants Rätrot was the last. Indeed, it had been Rätrot who had sold the very last Giltretch landholdings for a pittance, then fled to Schleswig's more disreputable quarters to drink up the last of his inheritance. In spite of these misfortunes, Rätrot consoled himself with the thought that, despite it all, a Giltretch still drew breath to see the Dancing Plague. That was more than could be said for the defunct and mostly-forgotten likes of contemporary families like Alberink, or Rutten, or Königsmann. All of those once-elated names now moldered under churchyards in decrepit ghost towns.

Rätrot did not want to be burned on a mass pyre. Nor

did he want to lie in some forgotten cemetery in the Totholz Forest. Rätrot, as it happened, didn't want to die of the Dancing Plague at *all.* Before he paid the hackman what was left of his silver, Rätrot had already laid his plans. He'd had a very special coffin built; then, he'd paid a miserly sum to his miserable retainer (whose father's father had served Rätrot's father's father) for one last act of service. Though hardly eager to perish of Parsifal's Polska himself, this retainer—Hadrian, by name—had a wife and family anchoring him to Schleswig, whereas Rätrot had only his own waxen hide to think of.

And waxen he was. As the last Giltretch reclined in his coffin to prepare for his escape, Hadrian could not help but note that his longtime employer played the corpse well, without benefit of greasepaint or powder. The placid, broad-faced servant had placed the final piece of Rätrot's gambit; a snug bandana filled with strong-scented herbs, fixed over Rätrot's narrow nose and pinched lips. Until the hackman's carriage stopped in Stimmen Cemetery, deep within the Totholz Forest, Rätrot would be stacked inside a slowly-moving warehouse of the dead. Though he didn't dare admit it to himself, Rätrot feared his great escape might prove as deadly as remaining locked behind Schleswig's walls.

"Are you sure . . . " Hadrian had begun.

"I *am,*" snapped Rätrot, crossing both his palms over his breast to better fit. "Now seal me up!"

The hammer's gentle taps were sharp against the silence of the predawn Schleswig air, but Rätrot hadn't had much time to worry about that detail. Mere moments after Hadrian had hammered the last nail home, the soft *clop-clop* of hooves could be heard on the lane.

"Good luck, Master Giltretch," Hadrian had whispered as Reiter and his hack came clopping slowly down the street.

Rätrot had held as still as death as Hadrian and the muttering hackman loaded him aboard. The carriage made another stop or two, and other coffins soon were loaded onto his. The stowaway breathed more easily, his fear of discovery diminished with each coffin taken on. *Easier to get lost in a crowd*, he thought.

Rätrot breathed with even greater ease once he felt the bouncing cobbles of Schleswig turn to rutted mud beneath the carriage wheels. He allowed himself a moment's silent celebration: he'd successfully escaped from Schleswig's pestilent embrace.

The coffin fit his long, lean frame as tightly as a wooden overcoat. His breath was loud within its confines, but muffled by the rag of herbs clapped to his face. The mixture smelled acrid, with a vaguely spoiled and meaty note beneath the tangy chords of herbage. Despite the vapors of this mephitic bouquet, Rätrot could not help but smell his traveling companions. In and of itself, this was nothing new; rare were the carriage journeys he had taken without one or more malodorous companions. These latest were quieter than most, but the stench of death was towering and monstrous. It filled the carriage like a vengeful thundercloud, a reeking, cheesy odor undershot by a malefic saccharinity; an odor like a dollop of sweet cream atop a dish of day-old tripe.

He tried to focus on his other senses, but in the dark, confining coffin, what was left to him was sound. The one he'd commissioned was less insulated than those sold for normal burial. It also was possessed of cleverly-disguised grates which admitted air and let its tenant hear the goings-on around him. Rätrot was justifiably proud of its design. Even the square-headed nails that Hadrian had hammered home were half as long as ordinary coffin nails, the better to allow Rätrot to burst forth and make his escape once the dead-man's carriage reached its destination.

He listened. The corpses boxed around him jostled gently and irregularly knocked against the sides of their enclosures with muted, hollow thumps as the hack surmounted ruts and stones along the road. Though they were closed, these treasure chests attracted eager flies. Soon the carriage was beset by a great, buzzing swath of them, and their demoniacal drone grated on his nerves.

"Soon," Rätrot murmured to himself. "This all will be over soon."

Folded in one of his coat's pockets was a crude map, which, if the man he'd stolen it from had not been a liar, sketched the Totholz trails between Stimmen Cemetery and the dubious freedom of the open Wastland. There, he'd try his luck anew. Perhaps he'd even shed the Giltretch name entirely (for all the good that it had done him). All he had to do, he told himself, was put up with the smell and his unpleasantly close confines for the nonce.

"Yes. Over soon," he said.

What happened next was probably inevitable. Perhaps it was the motion of Rätrot's mouth against the rag; perhaps it was the presence of a veritable feast of flies. More likely (though he didn't know it and he never would), it was the fact that Hadrian had purchased these "most efficacious herbs," as they'd been labeled, from a woman who had lost her mind. This alleyway apothecarist spent her nights collecting ingredients for her concoctions in the dark, web-shrouded catacombs beneath Schleswig; a place no sane person would explore for silver, let alone for strange vegetation.

Whatever combination of these factors was the cause, the result was an astonishing surprise to Rätrot: a clutch of groping, spindly legs came scuttling from the bundle clasped to his face, embracing his pale flesh with scabrous, scrabbling desperation.

The things he had awakened were indigenous to Schleswig's rotting catacombs, and if Rätrot had glimpsed them, it would hardly have improved his opinion. Each looked like an irregularly-legged cross between a centipede and spider. They were white as milk but for their clustered eyes, which glittered black with hideous intelligence.

Rätrot filled his pants with piss, and his coffin with the sound of muffled screams. He lifted both his hands, which had been clasped across his breast, and began to slap at his arthropod-adorned cheeks, brow, and neck. A tickle at the edge of one ear broke the dam of sane control and brought *true* panic. His wooden ticket out of Schleswig constrained his movements, and, unable to flee, Rätrot thrashed. He beat his head against the coffin lid so hard that it would have popped loose—had there not been more fully-laden caskets stacked atop it. As it was, he jammed his body desperately from side to side, too terrified and filled with scarlet-edged revulsion even to scream.

Rätrot had the meager satisfaction of feeling spiny bodies burst against the coffin's walls as his terrified convulsions intensified. His triumph was short-lived, however; his blood-smeared brow struck a final blow against the coffin lid with such ferocity that his vision filled with varicolored stars. Helpless, he descended into unconsciousness.

Meanwhile, atop the carriage's box, Reiter heard a lumping, thumping ruckus from the cab, but paid it little mind. He'd heard the same noise once or twice before, and was confident he knew its source; some hapless victim of the Japes, not quite expired, had drummed out their very last few heartbeats in their pall-cloaked, pine-planked prison. Reiter merely slipped the stained stem of his briar pipe between his lips, lit a withered spill from his hack's lantern-flame, and haloed his bascient in rolling clouds of smoke. In her traces, Grog let out a single, mournful whinny of reproach.

"Aye," Reiter agreed, affably enough. "'twill be the death of me one day."

Hearing returned to Rätrot first, but that was no surprise, given that he woke in total darkness. The stowaway's return to wakefulness was heralded by throbbing pain, which largely emanated his skull. By the sound of the hack's travels, they'd progressed deep into the Totholz Forest. No longer did his narrow pinewood casket resonate to the rutted and irregular bumps of wheels on dried mud ruts. However, neither did the wheels whisper over dry leaves, in the way he'd heard on previous carriage excursions through the woods.

A slow, regular creak and muffled thump was accompanied a rocking.It reminded him of rowboats on Lake Onda, but with the slosh and slap of water neatly excised. Rätrot had a sudden, vivid vision: Reiter's hack proceeding so deep into the Totholz Forest's hidden trails and long-forgotten pathways that the hardened earth and dried leaves of a well-trod road had become a spongy mat of pallid fungus. He could practically see the iron-rimmed wheels slick with slime, the undercarriage scraping over the hummocked mounds of moss left by the lost and long-unburied dead.

In such environs, Rätrot's mind suspected, the carriage would present an eerie sight. Reiter (*if it still* is *Reiter*, his mind whispered) perched atop his driver's box; the aging mare plodding, fetlock deep, through the rotting stew; and the ghastly quality the lantern's light would take on in such a deeply-shaded, ancient thicket. A mottled, swampy glow; a deep, mossy, green glow which would pulse and fade with every rocking, poorly-balanced turn of the wheels.

The next sound Rätrot's questing ears picked up caused him pause. He wondered for a moment if he was, in fact, still somnolent and dreaming, or suffering a side-effect of his crack to the head. For all the world, he thought he heard a *scheitholt*; an instrument his long-dead grandfather had played with proficiency. Rätrot himself had never learned to play. He'd sold the family's heirloom instrument for drink long years ago, but the sound he heard now, the sound of the long, wooden fingerboard and the peculiar vibrancy of its three waxed-linen strings, was *precisely* that of the *scheitholt* he had traded to his bristly-faced pawnbroker (and sometime fence). Its notes wove in and out of a distant, frantic reel of drums and pipes.

Rätrot concentrated—very hard—on waking up. Despite his best efforts, the coffin stayed enclosed around him; the air stayed dark as pitch and just as thick. He still heard the moss-galleon creak of Reiter's hack and, distantly, the out-of-key, frenetic reel.

Creaaaaak-knock. Creaaaaak-knock.

"You've lost your mind," he murmured to himself.

His voice, low as it was, seemed loud as thunder in the space around him. In such close confines, even his breath was loud. He tore the rag of herbs loose from his mouth, and a more bitter, hateful mouthful he could not imagine. At least the creeping things were dead, although the reek of their spoiled blood was rancid. His convulsive spasms seemed to have killed both the stowaway's stowaways and his fear at once.

Frankly, realizing he'd gone mad came as a relief, a sort of last surrender. "At least you picked a quiet place to do it," he said to himself. "Quiet, if a little short on company."

"Oh, I don't know about *that*," piped a voice that sounded like a genderless and strangely ageless child. "I'm *very* good company."

Rätrot screamed. He screamed without pride or reservation, a shrill, gobbling noise of shocked dismay. When his breath hitched back, he froze. He pictured Reiter's head turning, the eyes that glittered between his bascient fixing on his carriage: the carriage where his cargo should have been quite dead and well past screaming by that point.

Images floated through his mind like bubbles rising in a scummy pond; Reiter, dutiful to his arrangement, would halt the journey, step down from his box, and investigate. Perhaps he'd ram the long, ugly, triangular blade Rätrot had seen strapped to his belt through every coffin, just to be completely sure.

Creaaaaak-knock. Creaaaaak-knock.

"He won't bother us, oh no," the childlike voice went on. "You needn't worry. I'm here to talk and tell tales and maybe dance—will *you* dance? Oh *please*! Don't be fooled; there's room enough to make a lively step. Oh, my name is Pyg, by the by, and pleased to meet you, too!"

"Who . . . " Rätrot cleared his throat and gave his inquiry another go. "Who's there? Who are you?"

"We're the dead, you oaf." An old man's bored and self-important baritone rose from directly beneath Rätrot's casket; . Rätrot felt his bones vibrate with this speaker's sonorous proximity. "We're the dead of Schleswig, where we danced until our hearts gave out. Or our brains burst like the poked yolk of a soft-boiled egg. Or until our bones gave way and dropped us to the hard, uncaring street to break our necks."

Rätrot twitched, but this time didn't scream. He gnawed on what he'd heard. "Am *I* dead?" he asked, not quite sure how he felt about the idea. Remembering the remnant of his manners, he added quickly: "And you, sir? What is your name?"

The speaker from under him went silent as a gravestone, before finally saying, "Ookä is my name. And no, you're not dead. Though *I* died several days ago." Ookä paused, then went on meditatively. "On the whole I've found the torments of death to be a veritable *balm* compared to all that I endured in my long life. Particularly in the last few days of it."

"How you *capered*, Ookä!" This was another new voice—a third voice—and to Rätrot's heartbreak and his horror, one he recognized. One he knew quite well, in fact.

"Åste?" Rätrot gasped. Her name sucked all the breath from him in one great gust.

Åste Gheest and he had been as thick as thieves (metaphorically and literally) not that long ago. This was while Rätrot still had coin enough to buy strong drink for pretty girls. Despite his vulturine intent, it had been she who drank him blind, then stripped him of his gaudy, largely-worthless "valuables" as an encore performance. Her first feat left him comatose for most of the following day, and when he'd finally regained his wits, he'd tracked her down . . . but not for revenge.

It was love at first feint-riposte, and they'd become partners in petty theft as well as lovers. When their bond at last broke beneath the weight of life's inescapable downward trajectory in Schleswig, it had cut Rätrot deeply. Deeply enough to bleed his soul, and he had tried to staunch the flow by drinking up the last dregs of his ill-gotten gains.

He'd been engaged in that sad pastime when the pirouetting specter and harbinger of plague first appeared in Schleswig. Then, the Dancing Plague began to spread, and even *he'd* become aware of the unfolding peril. He'd heard, in some low, rotgut-serving public house, that Åste had been part of a great throng who'd dropped dead in a plaza called Somberl Square.

Had he wept? No, he had not. By then, his heart had hardened over twice; once from love and once from death. All the sentiment he could summon was a vague sense of encroaching loneliness. Needlessly, so it would seem; for wasn't she *here? Now?* In the back of Reiter's wagon of the dead among the coffins stacked four deep? On some forsaken, mossy path, slowly being hauled toward the hungry soil of Stimmen Cemetery?

"It's me, my poor, lost Baron Giltretch," said Åste in the same smile-laden, teasing tones she'd used in their familiar moments. "I'm here, too. I capered twice as hard as Ookä did, great lump that he was. And, eager dancer that *I* was. You remember, don't you, Rätrot?"

Gone mad, Rätrot thought again. (*A lie*, whispered a deeper self, *and furthermore, you* know *it is a lie.*) *A dream, or a contrivance of horror sprung by drink*, he thought. (*You know the feeling of those, don't you?* whispered Rätrot's deeper voice. *Does this feel like such a fancy?* It did not.)

"Shut up. You're dead," said Rätrot in a numb and stony whisper. "Dead and burned. I . . . "

A memory streaked through his mind like an ill-omen falling star. The memory was just as unwelcome as it was vivid; inscribed in hot engraver's acid into Rätrot's mind. He'd seen them burn the bodies taken from Somberl Square. They'd still believed they could control the plague's progression through the city, in those dim and distant days. Watching the Somberl bodies burn, Rätrot had picked out Åste's pale features from the other corpses. How could he have not, knowing her well-loved face far better than he knew his own? He'd seen that face grow thunderous with wroth. He'd looked into it in the throes of love. Then he saw it crisp and melt until it was a mutely shrieking, withered nub of a blackened skull. He hadn't looked away until the brightness of the flames threatened to burn his eyes. In the end, he'd seen the last of her meld with the ashen dead, borne upon a hurricane of flame into the evening sky.

Fire, he had thought, *is a great leveler. Aristocrat or thief, we all blow in the wind as ash together.* There'd been absolutely no comfort in the thought. Much more, he felt a sense of grim and helpless doom.

"I watched you burn," Rätrot finished.

"The dead go where the dead will," whispered Åste, and this time the words seemed to come from the inside of Rätrot's coffin, inches from his ear.

He shrieked with fright, fetching his aching head another whack against the coffin's lid, which was still held firmly closed by the corpse-weight piled atop his camouflaged conveyance.

A low, ponderous chuckle came from the baritone-voiced wraith beneath him; the one who'd called himself Ookä. "Certainly," said Ookä with rich, pine-vibrating amusement. "The dead go where the dead will, don't we, little Pyg?"

Pyg giggled. The child's unsettling titter had a clicking

and percussive undertone. It took Rätrot a moment to realize that the sound was teeth; Pyg's teeth chattering like dice as the dead little mouth gave unwholesome birth to cruel-edged mirth.

"The dead go where the dead will," echoed Pyg, and added: "Isn't that why you make your passage here with us today? Many trapped in Schleswig have died dancing to the pipes of death. Many more have died as cowards, murderers, or desperate fools. But *you*, Rätrot, only *you* were willing to pay the toll no one else would."

The hack's sodden, slumping pace degenerated to a drunken lurch. Rust-bound bolts squealed where, previously, the wheels had rolled along smooth and even.

When and why had things deteriorated so? At least . . . that was, if this *was* still Reiter's hack. But where else *could* he be? Had Reiter effected some sort of middleman exchange while Rätrot lay unconscious in his box? No; just as surely as he knew Åste's voice when he heard it, he felt he was, in at least some sense, still in the same conveyance.

Some sense, Rätrot thought with kindled dread, *encompasses a plentitude of meanings in the dark of Totholz Forest.*

He had a sudden terrible vision of a carriage whose every surface was weighed down with forest moss, dappled with abundant tomb mold, driven by a skeletal hackman. Perhaps one whose unceasing rictus grim gleamed below a bascinet helm half-holed with black corrosion. And drawn by something terrible, which wore a pale, sore-riddled horse's skin draped over its bloated, multilegged form.

"Oh yes," repeated Ookä. "To pay the toll."

"Shut up," Rätrot choked, digging hard for bravery. "I'll not be menaced by some moth-eaten *shade*."

"But my Duke . . . You paid the toll. To take the road," Åste replied. This time, her voice came from above him, near what must have been the pinnacle of this unwieldy coffin-load.

"*What* road? Where are we *going*?" Rätrot cried. His voice struck his own ears as very high and very shrill within the angular confines of his coffin.

From somewhere outside, in what must have been the deepest depths of Totholz Forest, the swirling skirl of pipes played on. The waxed strings of the *scheitholt* sang, and now Rätrot was certain it *was* the antique he'd sold; his grandfather and father's beloved instrument. But it wasn't just the instrument he recognized. The song—the ballad of someone-or-other the something-or-other; he had never paid the words much mind—was one both men had played, and as he listened, Rätrot could have sworn the player's style shifted from one to the other, and back again.

Another rattling giggle made him start. "*The road of the dead; the dancers, the bled,*" chanted Pyg, as though it were a nursery song worn smooth as a stream's pebbles by years of repetition. "*Out with your sweetmeats and off with your head!*"

"Shut *up*," Rätrot gasped. It ended in a ragged sob. "*Please!*"

"Ah, but every journey has to end." Åste's soft, flirtatious murmur came from just beside him again, but this time panic didn't take him when he heard her.

It took him when he *felt* her. First her freezing breath against the inside of his soft cochlear shell, and then her cold, dead tongue working its slimy, grit-flecked way deeply into his ear canal.

"And when a journey's over, every traveler needs a place to stay," said Ookä with rancid generosity. "We'll prepare a place for you, last son of the Giltretch Barony. It's only right that royalty should keep each other company."

Not that Ookä spoke for Rätrot's benefit; his screams had died abruptly as his mind gave way, and he took refuge in unconsciousness.

COFFIN BERTH

Reiter hauled back on the reins, neatly bringing his hack and its freight to a halt on the far edge of Stimmen Cemetery. Its wheels were true and quiet, and its black sides were home to neither mold nor moss. Reiter puffed his pipe as he descended from the box, unfurling a long banner of ivory smoke. It hung and hovered in the still, moist air. Grog, his swaybacked mare and primary companion of countless years, gave an appreciative snort and bent her head to graze.

"Aye," agreed Reiter, running a callused palm down her flank. "I'm glad to be here again, too."

Reiter liked the Totholz Forest. He knew its reputation to be fearsome, and he'd heard enough firsthand accounts to steer wide of the hungry powers lurking in its lightless depths. Yet, at the same time, in its shaded paths and secret places, he felt a sense of profound peace. He didn't view these two truths as a contradiction: he held Totholz Forest in polite esteem and high respect and, so far, had been treated likewise in return. As Grog cropped her dinner, he added clouds of sweet tobacco smoke to the forest's ambient banks of mist. Finally, he clamped the briar pipe between his teeth and pulled his pick and shovel from the carriage boot.

Digging graves in Schleswig was not a job for one gravedigger. Reiter knew this from experience; he'd worked as a sexton in two separate boneyards during his tenure there, picking up the jobs when the carriage business slowed from time to time. That had been hard, brutal work. Digging graves in Stimmen Cemetery wasn't like that; not at *all*. The soft soil yielded easily to pick and spade, and never threw a rock or root to turn aside one's efforts. It was, Reiter reflected, as though the long-forgotten graveyard *hungered* for more tenants.

Nor was Stimmen's black, rich loam eager to give up

its dead once they were seated there. Once a grave was filled in Stimmen Cemetery, little trace of burial remained, unless one left a sturdy marker. Reiter didn't offered headstone services to his clients. Placing them would simply take too long and weigh too much.

His steady efforts were paced perfectly. Just as he was packing soil firmly on the grave of his last charge, the swollen sun dipped its lower edge below the treetops. Much as he may have loved the peace of Totholz Forest, only those beset by madness (or sorcerous intent) would brave the woods at night.

Reiter looked upon the new graves, puffed his pipe, and quietly philosophized. His inclinations in this regard would not have surprised a soul in Schleswig; it was well known there that all sextons and all carriage drivers were philosophers, which made him such twice over.

"Death's a funny thing, Grog," he said. The mare twitched an ear as though to say *go on, but let me graze as you pontificate: I think best while I chew*. "Death's a funny thing, because every soul who lives exists in fear of it, and they spend their time devising stratagems to avoid it or, at least, avoid thinking about it. But there's naught to fear. Just facts we must accept. The young. The old. The ones we love. Death comes for them all." He shrugged, but Grog gave him an approving grunt.

Before he mounted his now-empty carriage, Reiter paused to look upon the time-corroded stones that *did* mark graves in Stimmen Cemetery. These were the families who'd died while it had still seen frequent clientele, and though a combination of pallid moss and time endeavored to erase all trace of them, the names could still be read. He ticked them off one by one, poking at their legends with his pipestem.

"Alberink," he said to Grog. "Rutten. Königsmann. Well, 'king's-man' or not, Fathmu IV showed *that* one little mercy, in his day." He took a deep draw on his pipe, rolled the smoke around his tongue, and spat with feeling onto the last grave in the triptych. "*Thus* to all your wretched breed," he said, and turned back to his carriage. From atop its box he added: " . . . and it's a *pleasure* to bury your spawn here in your obscurity. I'd have done the job for half the price."

This valediction delivered, Reiter took up Grog's reins and gave them a tired flap. *A brisk day's work*, he thought, wincing at the twinges in his joints, *but a rich one*. His hack rolled on its sturdy wheels, creaking gently back up the trail; no shrieking, rusted bolts, no swamp-green lantern light, and only Reiter riding it.

All his other passengers—most of them dead—were behind him, buried in the soft, voracious soil of Stimmen Cemetery. The loam there was forever hungry, as it whispered to those who would listen. As it had whispered, in fact, to Reiter when he'd found it, some years back. Forever hungry for new voices, and with eternal room to spare.

The hackman drove his rig away as Rätrot Giltretch woke inside his coffin, buried deeply in the heavy, night-black loam. He wasn't awakened by the sound of voices, though they rushed about him like the wind he'd never feel again. Nor was it the song of pipes accompanied by an antiquated, linen-stringed instrument wielded with some skill.

No, what woke Rätrot was a ragged, jagged twitching in his legs, followed shortly by a grinding of his teeth as his jaws locked into a rictus grin.

His resting place was darker than the dirt itself, but if a witness saw the fallen baron's eyes, they'd know the cruelest part of Rätrot's fate. The knife's twist was that he faced his death wide awake, and fully cognizant of what was happening.

In his grave, Rätrot began to dance.

In time that would seem endless to him, he'd begin to die.

THE KNIGHT AND THE BEAST

ZAC GOINS

"IT'S A WASTELAND. Barren as your sister."

"I know what it's *supposed* to be. Just not seen it for myself, is all. Perhaps it's a bit more than that."

"It couldn't possibly be more than that. The soil's dead. The water's dead. Trees are dead. Dead to the last. Nothing grows. Hell, nothing even lasts. Hence the idea of a wasteland."

"But aren't valleys supposed to be fertile? Can't be both fertile and barren, and if your name says you're fertile, then I don't think you can also be barren."

"It might have been fertile in some past life, but more than age has took that valley. It's long past the point of bearing any life."

"But what about the sn—"

"Oh, you're a fool, and I'm a fool for humoring you."

From the shadows that dance across the opposite side of the sputtering campfire, another voice joins the duo. "Both of ye, *hush*."

Three sets of ears prick up. Three heads turn this way and that. The bitter wind whips around the stone overhang and slaps against them, showing more vigor than the fire. Wool blankets are pulled tighter. The wind offers no council or warning, save for its own.

"Did you hear something, then?" This comes from the smallest of the knights, Rupert, a short, husky fellow with sharp eyes, small teeth, and a black cloak tipped with wolf's fur. A sheathed sword and a solid board are propped up against his pack beside him.

"Only the sound of your wheezing and ignorant mewling." This voice belongs to someone altogether more knightly in stature. A noble in every sense of the word, other than the truest, for the surname Hamfast has never held land or office. Bruckard is the closest thing his line ever held to nobility.

Even now, his long build stretches full beside the small fire, his legs alone accounting for most of the height of his dwarfish companion. A shield assists a pack in propping up his torso. A spear with an iron head is in his hands.

The third knight speaks. "No, it was more than the wind."

He stands, and the others follow him.

"Listen."

It starts out at the edge of senses. One could be forgiven for mistaking it for a whispered moan of the wind.

The third knight places a finger to his lips, warding off any commentary.

The wind carries the sound down the mountain, dancing and twisting off rocks and nearly muffled by snow. By the time it reaches their ears, it is a pitiful thing . . . but it is certainly not just the wind.

Finally, Bruckard speaks, "That's it."

The third knight picks up a stout crossbow, pressing its stock into his shoulder. "Aye. It is."

Rupert ducks, scraping up his sword and board, kicking out the fire in a swift motion. It hisses and pops in a half-hearted fight against the snow, ice, and wind. When it dies, the darkness is complete, and the wind claims its victory with another gleeful gust.

The knights bundle their gear and shoulder their packs in a moment. They take turns tightening the straps on each other's armor. Bruckard pats the icon of the twin gulls emblazoned upon Rupert's breastplate, then his own, and then briefly touches the final knight's.

"By our Lady's bidding," he says.

"For her waxen seal and silver coin," Rupert responds, shaking his limbs to awaken his blood.

The third knight's expression is impassive, and his eyes have yet to stray from the upper mountain. With the wind-scattered snow swirling, the total darkness that comes with this far north, and the ever-present churn of clouds, he cannot hope to see further than a few strides, if that. Only the glistening, packed snow and ice offer any light, reflecting . . . well, the man isn't sure, really. Perhaps it is the light of the hidden stars pushing their way through. Or perhaps it is a memory of the moon's gleam, like how a brand remembers the light of its furnace. Or perhaps it is the Lady's magic, extending even here. Her pale, cold touch, caressing the tips of her kingdom, stealing its warmth, but leaving her anemic signature. Perhaps the wind is, in truth, her long exhalation.

The man has seen Her breath in person. Watched as She inhaled, and the life-breath of a kneeling, pubescent youth was torn from their lips.

In times of reason, life-breath slips out quietly and without color. Not so in Lady Anthelia's court. There, it is drawn as by a leech, emerging red and as a mist. As it is drawn, the child's body topples, and the Lady rises in turn. She strides down the steps from her throne and enters the red. It bathes her, and she welcomes it. It draws into her, giving a momentary flush to her cheeks and warmth to her skin. She gasps the gasp of a lover in ecstasy. Shivers. Those of her court avert their eyes.

All too quickly, the warmth fades and the flush gives way to cold ivory once more. The countess sighs and the cold that comes from her mouth has a chill that causes the dogs to tremble. She turns back to her throne.

The body is removed, and another is made ready for

the morrow. All of this a scene played daily for as long as anyone can remember. The court is quiet through it all.

Upon the mountain, Bruckard coughs and Rupert shuffles his feet. The third knight—once a member of the royal guard, former bearer of a ruby-pommeled blade, now gaunt, grim, and hunched—is turned from his memory.

The conclusion to the informal creed of the Kergün military is drawn from him. "May her favor lift us higher than her gaze may see."

"Wickheads!" the third knight calls in warning.

Through blinding light, the sound of a gear releasing chuffs, followed by a wet *thwack*.

"On your left!" Rupert barks as he pitches forward, pounding the flat of his blade against his shield to mark his location.

"Fall back!" Bruckard commands, pressing his board against the third knight's shoulder.

The knight gives way, and a second shield is placed at the forefront, a spear jutting out as a further barrier.

The lights, as bright as bullseye lanterns, flash ahead, bouncing as the wickheads press for an opening.

On the left, a larger light surges. Rupert lets out a cry as he sees the flash of steel and shifts his shield just in time to catch the arching swing of a dented blade.

There is a crank of gears, and the third knight calls, "A moment longer."

Two more swords streak out of the light, both deftly caught on shields.

A spear darts forward, causing two of the lights to dance back.

As the knights' eyes begin adjusting to the light, they avoid looking directly towards their foes, instead searching the boundaries of the searing glare for the suggestion of gear or limbs.

Again, Rupert barks, "Five! Four slenders and a beast!"

"Keep low," comes the follow up, and the two shield-bearers instinctively duck.

Another gear releases as the crossbow lets loose a bolt. This one slams into the center mass of the largest light, extinguishing it in an instant.

The other lights flare and press forward. Though no battle cries sound, the desire for revenge is evident. Three swords impact the wood and steel of the knights' shields, but a fourth slips through, causing Bruckard to grunt and stumble to one knee.

In an instant, four wickheads swarm him, blades swatting against armor, piercing into flesh.

Rupert smells the sulfur, chokes from the fumes, but wades in nonetheless, hacking at wickhead flesh, bone, and wax. The third knight joins him, swinging his reversed crossbow like a club and cracking into the shoulder of an enemy.

A light dims.

Another disappears entirely.

Voice low, Bruckard sounds angry and desperate. "Get 'em off me!"

A thrust of Rupert's blade extinguishes the dimmed light. Two remain.

Sensing the tide has turned, the survivors backpedal, dousing their own lights and plunging the cave back into darkness, blinding the knights yet again. Only the sound of their retreating footsteps can be heard.

"Don't let 'em escape!" calls Rupert, charging onto the steep and narrow pathway.

The third knight hurries close behind, while Bruckard struggles to his feet, teeters, and then collapses against the cave wall, bleeding from a dozen gashes. "Give 'em . . . " he wheezes, then coughs and spits. "Give 'em the boot!" as his body slackens.

Rupert doesn't hear, so focused is he on his targets and so terrible is the howl of the wind around him. It doesn't matter, regardless.

The path cuts back, a sharp turn to avoid a deadly plunge. Both wickheads make the turn, the last embers of their wicks giving off a minutia of light.

Rupert ignores the turn altogether, casts aside his shield, and leaps from above into the body of the leading enemy. Producing a wicked phurba from its sheath, he plows into his target. The blade does its deadly work, plunging over and over, spraying hot blood and tallow.

He rides the creature to the ground and then throws himself aside as the wickhead, desperate to be rid of its stinging mount, rolls too far and plunges off the cliff-face, into the swirling darkness below.

In return, the final wickhead brings its sword down onto Rupert's exposed right arm. There's an audible snap, another spray of blood, and the knight lets out a full cry of pain. He recoils, pressing his arm against his side, only then realizing that his forearm and hand are left behind, severed cleanly at the elbow. He lets out another shriek.

Ever the more cautious, the third knight turns the corner. He too has cast aside his initial gear and drawn a knife.

The wickhead raises its sword again—a promised end to its cowering victim.

With a cry, the approaching knight throws his knife and strikes the back of its hand. Involuntarily, it drops the sword, turning to its attacker, its head flaring back to life.

But a royal guard will only be caught once by the same gambit—too often are their minds sharpened by the politics of court.

A hatchet is already in his hand as the wickhead turns and ignites its lantern head. It raises its empty hands to ward off the blow, but the blade knows its path and will not be denied.

The first hack chops through an arm like kindling.

The second, the hatchet finds purchase in the narrow neck. With the third, the hatchet cleaves into bone. The knight grips the wickhead's heated bronze helm and delivers a final strike.

The headless body topples, leaving the knight holding the still-gleaming light.

Some time later, having hauled the pain-delirious Rupert from the cliffside, the knight applies bandages and salves to his companions' wounds. The cave now clear, it delivers now on the false-promise it had implied before; namely, some amount of security and no small amount of shelter from the elements.

With both Rupert and Bruckhard fallen into an exhausted sleep, the royal guard sets to further securing the area. Little can be done about the mouth of the cave, for it is far too wide to barricade with anything in their packs.

A war can only be won on one front at a time, whispers the battle-training in his mind.

He turns to survey the deeper parts of the cave, using the still-flickering head as a torch. By some unnatural and unreasonable phenomenon, a wickhead alit at the moment of death will continue to shed light until it is by intent extinguished.

This is one of the few bits of fortune the man can recall in recent memory. He tries to think back to his last bit of fortune . . .

The lucky hand he drew last week? Nay, that ended in a brawl that smarted in his jaw and teeth even still.

The bit of coin they had earned doing a side venture on the Sarkash border a few weeks previous? Hard to call coin fortunate when it's earned. Besides, that was the sort of nasty business best left forgotten; he had made a vow in the moment to never take on such a venture again, and mostly he meant it.

Certainly, nothing fortunate could be said of the months before that, for they culminated in his expulsion from the guard and all the shit that came after.

Dimly, he can remember a time when he spent his evenings and off-duty hours tucked into a corner near a hearth, with a bowl of stew, a warm cloak, and paid-but-pleasant company at his call. He didn't see that as fortune back then, but he certainly does now.

With the thought, regret threatens to choke him, so he turns his attention back to matters at hand.

The cave appears devoid of any other inhabitants, as far as he can tell. The ceiling dips sharply further in, leaving only a crack between it and the floor. Altogether, the livable space is no more than twenty meters deep, and never wider than four.

Something catches his interest in one of the larger recesses. A large mound of wax houses assorted items, immersed within layers of the solidified substance.

The knight carefully strips away wax with the edge of his hatchet, in the same way that a carpenter uses a hand plane to shape wood. He uncovers a small, wooden case and a silver mirror wrapped in an oil cloth.

Time slips by as the man carries on clearing the wax, unearthing more tantalizing hints as he goes.

Bruckard awakens, hacks up a mouthful of phlegm and blood, and attempts to stand, bracing a hand on the cave wall to sturdy himself. He glimpses the lantern light reflecting deeper in the chamber and stumbles forward, using his spear as a cane.

"What's to be found?" he asks as he nears his busy companion.

The third knight gestures to the mess surrounding him. Chunks of hewn wax mixed and bits of rubble and debris are scattered about; a few items have been placed to the side. A corpse dressed in fine velvets and furs has been unearthed, as have the remains of a leather pack and a staff.

"I'm guessing this is what's left of those alands' master."

Bruckard eases himself down. "I didn't know they had a master."

"Not all do now, but they all did at the beginning. Every craft must have a craftsman behind it. I've even heard that there's a maker's mark on the better ones."

"Any marks on the ones we killed?"

"Not that I can see. I did find something better, though."

Bruckard pauses his perusal of the found items. "And what's that?"

His companion grins and dumps out the leather pack, spilling forth some rock-hard rations, a torn wineskin, a small coin pouch that promises no measurable wealth, firesteel, and two tubular cases made of fine leather and embroidered in delicate runes.

At the sight of the cases, Bruckard gasps.

"Scrolls!" he whispers, awe heavy in his voice.

"Aye, scrolls. Haven't given them an open yet, but I'm hopeful. The pack looked unspoiled, save by time."

Possibilities danced in the minds of both men.

"I also haven't looked in that case next to you yet."

The wooden box is no larger than what might hold a sewing kit. Bruckhard glances over at the still-sleeping Rupert. "Do we want to wait for him?"

"He won't do us much good in his current state if anything was to happen."

"Fair point," Bruckard says, lifting the case and gauging its weight. "Too light for coin."

"And we've also got a purse."

"Aye." Bruckard eases the hinged lid open. A low whistle escapes his lips, sending him into another coughing fit.

A trio of small, glass bottles are tucked inside, nestled in velvet. Each contains no more than a single swallow of a red liquid that shifts and sways in its vessel, even though his steady hand offers no movement.

"By all that's divine . . . " Bruckard remarks.

"Elixirs then," the other man agrees excitedly. "Couldn't ask for better fortune." Bruckard carefully places the lid back in place and looks toward the scroll cases, his hands trembling. "Now for them."

"I'll take the heat this time," offers the other.

"Don't read 'em," Bruckard says. "Just a peek for a hint or two."

His companion nods and releases the latch on the first case. Both men wait, motionless, as if anticipating some sort of arcane response. But none presents itself.

The knight slides a hand in and slowly draws forth a roll of parchment. Both men gasp; this is the first time they have seen such a potent thing up close, let alone in hand.

The parchment is thick and showcases a vermilion luster.

"A red spell," Bruckard remarks, as if possessing some knowledge that the coloration of a scroll indicates its contents.

His companion nods solemnly and unrolls a small length. Both men avert their gaze and but are quickly drawn back to peer at what the dried ink might indicate. Luckily, no letters are yet in view; they have heard that, if anyone dares to read even a few words of power, they must immediately contend with the arcane will bound within and see the reading through to the end. Success might allow the harnessing of said power, but failure would undoubtedly be catastrophic.

But only the filigree and decorum are visible, and both men gaze upon it in rapture. A dozen, dozen illustrated eyes gaze back, gracing the page in all manner of sizes. Most appear violent, their pupils but pinpricks, flames dancing both within and without.

After a moment, Bruckard says, "Probably an understatement, but that doesn't look like a good one."

"I agree, unfortunately," the other man responds, sliding the scroll back into its case.

Turning to the second, he unclasps its latch, removes the lid, and dumps the scroll into his hand.

It is made from the same red-sheened parchment.

Again, they peer at its first section with furtive eyes. This one has a rising sun centered at the top, the rays extending toward both sides. As they look, the ink appears to catch the light, shifting between black and a brilliant yellow.

"A sun. Not altogether unwholesome, especially in this place," Bruckard states.

The other nods. "Maybe we chance a fuller look?"

Bruckard hesitates, scooting away without fully rising. "I don't know that I'm up for it, but I won't stop you," he says.

The other nods again and takes a step away from his companion before unrolling the scroll further. He turns his back so that Bruckard won't risk an accidental glance and unrolls the scroll further.

"There's a chariot pushing through some clouds . . . all the ink shifts and changes . . . "

Bruckard continues inching away. Shadows press in. The lantern's light fights to maintain dominance.

"Perhaps that's enough of a look."

The knight does a quick glance over his shoulder before turning back to the scroll, "What good is power if we don't know its form?" the knight asks.

Bruckard doesn't answer, save to backpedal another few steps back toward the entrance.

Turning back to his parchment, the knight's shoulders tense as if in heavy concentration.

And then it happens.

A shrill blast erupts from the scroll, ripping the air asunder, and filling the cave with a sudden heat. The third knight's startled cry mutates into a guttural incantation. Light pours from the parchment, absorbing and dwarfing the light from the deceased wickhead.

"Stop!" orders Bruckard, now nearly to Rupert. From his vantage, he can only see the silhouette of the other knight's form, and half the glowing parchment. It looks like the sun now and fills the entire space with light.

He doesn't stop. Can't stop. His words ring out in the brilliance with an energy all their own. Bruckard shakes Rupert, but the man is deep in his own darkness and does not stir.

"Damn this place!" Bruckard cries.

As if in answer, the light begins to pulse, and the intensity of its heat causes snowdrifts at the cave mouth to hiss in pain. The knight's voice rises to a crescendo that threatens to shake loose the mountain crags. Bruckard marvels through his fear, for he has never heard such potency in his companion's voice—nay, in anyone's!—before. It sounds as if it belongs to an elder being that had long since cast this word aside in favor of another. It sounds like the voice of blessed creation but hemmed on all sides with the promise of coming damnation.

It sounds like the voice of a god.

And then the god-voice falters, mortal tongue and frost-bit lips failing to keep pace with the requisite words.

The light goes dark, before rushing back with a harsh, red gleam.

His voice finally freed, the third knight lets out a cry of terror and drops the parchment, stumbling toward the entrance as if pushing against a strong wind.

For a moment, Bruckard considers rushing to his aid. The next moment, however, ceases such thought.

Whatever force resists the knight becomes ultraviolent, as if tiring of the resistance muscle and bones make against it, propelling the man back toward the scroll with tremendous power and peeling back hair and flesh like a flaying knife in the hands of an adept butcher. The knight screams as his lips are wrenched from his face, along with his cheeks, eyelids, and other bits of flesh.

From within, his form bulges and swells. Organs press against ribs and push aside muscle, bloating like bloody balloons before bursting in sprays of ichor that are drawn into the scroll alongside the flayed flesh. Muscles rip loose with a tearing sound that sends shivers down Bruckard's back. Eyes tear from sockets and are chased into the scroll by whatever other remnants of flesh or organs remain.

Having gorged itself fully, the light from the scroll

fades, dissolves, and leaves the knight's bare skeleton clattering to the floor.

Bruckard eases his way back into the chamber, terrified of disturbing any remnant magic the scroll might contain. He thinks better of it and turns to Rupert, attempting to shake him awake once more.

Only now does he notice the stiffness to Rupert's form, the wide pool of red, and the cold of his dead flesh.

"No," he says, pleading with the Basilisks, or whatever forgotten gods there may still be, to deny fate this one occurrence.

A prayer escapes his lips as he falls to his knees. "I beg of you, all who are holy and just, do not forsake me here. First of all mothers, SHE, heed my cry. Close your ears to HIS wrath and do not heed the bitter desire of HE who nuzzles at your breasts. You who would deny the world, deny fate its victory here. Look down upon your servants, your children, and spit your blessing upon my companion. If ever you have looked upon us or our Lady with favor, I beg thee to heed my plea. Blessed be thy gaze, Lusi, and blessed are those who are caught in its splendor. *Låt det vara så.*"

With that, he swoons on his feet, overtaken by his fear, his wounds, and his despair. He falls, and as his body impacts the stone, another awakens . . . and rises.

When he revives, some time later—much later, if he were to hazard a guess—Bruckhard feels rested, but his body is stiff with dried blood and bandages. He's propped against the cave wall, and as he turns to his left, he sees a body covered with a blanket. He puts a hand on the chest to feel for movement or a heartbeat. Nothing. Dead then.

He closes his eyes. Opens them again, resigned to this truth, but grateful that at least one of them was spared.

"You there," he calls, seeing light in the back of the cave. "How long . . . how long have I been out?"

The voice that responds is not familiar. "Not long. Perhaps three hours." It sounds deep but hollow, more like an echo than a full sound.

"Who . . . who are you?" Thinking of the arcane items still lying in the cave, he adds, "Mind the scrolls! They've already done so . . . so much."

There's a pause. The sound of movement and the shift of light.

"Yes. Yes, indeed they have."

"Who are you?" Bruckard asks again. He feels in no way prepared for a fight, and determines, against all better judgment, to assume the voice belongs to a benevolent soul.

"I . . . I'm a friend. You can trust me."

"I call my friends by name. What is yours?"

A longer pause.

"Britvas."

Bruckard swallows. "Nay. I saw you fall. Saw your flesh ripped from your bones. The power . . . it tore you to pieces." He swallows again. "Unless . . . unless that was a dream."

" . . . It was not a dream."

The voice doesn't sound like Britvas. Doesn't sound like any person Bruckard would have ever called his friend.

"Be you a fiend? Or . . . or a specter of my companion, come to haunt this cavern?"

"Neither, but not altogether different from either. I will show you my form when you are ready."

Bruckard spots his spear against the opposite wall. Too far to be of any use. "I'm not sure I wish to see."

" . . . That may well be. But you begged HER, and I am HER answer. Would you deny HER blessing?"

Fear slips further into his stomach. "No."

"Then make yourself ready, for we have a task still to do."

With that, the light moves closer and Bruckard heard the footfalls of its bearer. A figure emerges from around the corner, and he beholds the horror that was once his companion.

Before him stands a skeleton stripped to bleach white,

with empty sockets and a dark, crackling energy binding bone to bone. In its left hand it carries the wickhead lantern, and in its right it holds a pack filled with gear, treasures, and the scroll cases.

Bruckard's hands begin to shake. His mouth goes dry. He tries to speak, to cry out, to deny it, but nothing emerges.

Certainly, he has seen his fair share of unholy beasts and desecrated corpses. Some years ago, he even dared to walk the outer rings of the Graven-Tosk, skewering more than a few shamblers that sought to drag him into an early grave. Once, he bore witness to a winged person with talons for feet and a mouth full of venom, dragged before the countess in the late-night hours. He remembers well that creature's shriek, and its unwholesome aura that made his stomach churn for days.

Yet he has never witnessed the denigration of one he has known, of a friend. One skull can hardly be recognized from another, but Bruckard is somehow certain he gazes upon the third member of his company, and that the shrouded body beside him is of the stout Rupert. To be certain, he pulls down the blanket and confirms the face, seeing two silver coins have been placed upon his eyes. The dead man's complexion is pale, but he looks peaceful.

"At least one of us should know peace," he whispers, covering again the form.

"Steel yourself, knight," commands the skeleton, its mouth opening and the echo-voice emitting from a mass of black energy within. "We have a beast still to hunt, and our Lady is waiting."

Near the peak of the mountain, the snow and rock give way to ice that rises in twisted spires. Long ago, druids had cut a network of homes and temples within the spires, furnishing their interiors with the pelts of cave bears, white foxes, and other creatures that dwelt on the mountainside.

The druids have long since died out or faded back to the forests of Sarkash. The mountain is a cold shoulder and a knife in the back to all, even those who insist on enjoying her company. The furs and furnishings of the homes and sacred spaces have long since fallen to ruin, and many of the spaces have become the dens of the very same creatures whose ancestors were skinned to adorn them.

Bruckard and the living skeleton have cleared several such dens but have yet to spy their quarry. They have come to the largest structure built into the tallest of spires. Like a mage's tower, it winds its way upward, with ice-hewn steps and brittle ladders. Numerous small rooms give way to even smaller rooms as the spire tapers.

Traces of the beast have been noticed: a shedding of fur here, a five-fingered claw mark there, Dates scratched in the permafrost walls, dried blood near the sign of a scuffle, the bones of a cave bear cast aside.

Only a single room remains, up a final ladder and into a heavily furred room beyond. The light of the lantern cannot reveal all, but as it casts its first rays, a shuffling noise followed by a single muffled bleat.

The skeleton calls out in a commanding tone, "Devil of SHE! Cast down and marked! Show yourself and submit, for you trespass within the kingdom of Kergüs and must answer to our Blood Countess, Lady Anthelia."

From above is only silence.

"Come down, damn it!" Bruckard says, hoping to avoid having to scale the ladder.

The bleating returns, almost as a laugh. "Damn it, indeed!" Words rasp through the animalistic chuckle. "Damn it all and damn yourself. Join your companion in damnation but damn me at your own peril."

The skeleton snorts—an odd sound to be sure—and raises its crossbow, slinging its pack to the ground.

Bruckard stays it with a gesture and shakes his head, producing a pair of manacles.

"We don't wish to kill you, beast," he says, "just to bring you before our Lady. Your fate will be up to her."

A dark shape looms near the opening through which

the ladder ascends. "You would do well to kill me. One step farther from damnation for us all."

"Be that as it may, it's not my intention."

"And what benefit shall my submission gain me?" The monstrous shape crouches, still removed enough from view that only the hint of detail can be parsed. One clawed hand reaches out and grips the opening's edge. Its nails are chipped and long and dig into the ice. Coarse black hair coats the forearm.

"As comfortable a journey as I can manage, my protection along the way, and a good word on your behalf upon our arrival." Bruckard offers up the manacles.

"A good word? How far do you imagine your word will extend, good knight? Will your word lessen your Lady's wrath? Will it quell the ignorant terror of all who look upon me? Will it stay the executioner's ax?"

Bruckard sighs. "Perhaps not, but it is better than lying dead here in the wasteland."

The laugh comes again, but quieter. Contemplative.

Bruckard determines to ride it out with patience.

Again, the beast speaks, quoting the Nameless Scriptures. "'Children winter-born and fated to fall before the snow, both shall it take . . . And the last King and the last Queen shall wither to dust. Their wretched courts are devoured by wolves. You shall know the last day is come. The sun shall set and never rise . . . and Anthelia shall have her will and drink all color from the world.' What a lovely future your good word will bring. What hope your Lady offers this dying world. Tell me, knight, have you ever wondered what the wolves are doing at court in the first place? Why aren't they in the wild?"

Bruckard shifts on his feet, still holding out the manacles. "I suppose I don't know. Are they meant to be nobles and courtesans?"

"Ha!" A fit of bleating laughter reverberates in the small space. "Of course, men would assume they are the wolves. You always hope to be your own demise."

Both hands now grip the edge, and the face manifests in the opening. Its long, goat-like, and twisted in a sneer. Its eyes are black with a touch of embers. Its teeth gnash, unnaturally sharp and wicked as a wolf's.

The skeleton guard raises its crossbow again, but the beast pays it no mind. Larger than a tall man, and both repulsive and awe-inspiring, it shows no fear.

"Heed my words, noble knight. You are not the wolves. Your court is not the wolves. Your countess is the only beast within your court. And, yes, she shall drain your world, but she shall not be alone in her ruination." One of the clawed hands rises sharply to point at Bruckard. "*You* are but her dogs. You run and pant and wag your tail and are blissful in your ignorance. It will be *you*, knight, who brings the first wolf into the paddock, and even now you beg for its company and offer it your comfort, and your protection, and your 'good word.'"

Bruckard pushes hard against the doubt that creeps into his mind. "I am only a man doing my Lady's bidding and attempting, beast, to be *reasonable* in my offering. I do not and cannot speak for the intentions or nature of others, leastwise yourself."

The skeleton says, "Drop down here, beast. Face your fate."

Now it is the beast's turn to snort. "I have faced it longer than your young lives already. Faced it and have determined to deny it."

Bruckard casts down the manacles and takes up his spear. "You may fell us, beast, but more will come."

The beast's forked tongue darts out like a snake's. "Yes, as it always is with man. There are always more of you. Always more until the last day." It withdraws its head back into the upper chamber. "I will descend and treat with you on your own level."

Both the knight and the skeleton take a step back and then another. "Very well," Bruckard says.

With a paltry amount of grace, the shaggy beast

descends the ladder on cloven hooves. It stoops to avoid its twin horns scraping the ceiling.

Bruckard holds his shield at the ready, and points to the manacles with the tip of his spear. "Bind yourself," he commands.

The beast picks up the manacles. "What you seek will be your undoing. What you set aflame cannot be undone. Are you so eager to see the last day?" When the knight gives no reply, it turns to the skeleton. "And what say you, former man? You have glimpsed ruin once already. Are you prepared to bring the same to kith and kin?"

"Damned if I heed the words of a beast," responds the skeleton.

The beast snarls. "Damned if you do, damned if you don't, it would seem."

"Isn't that the lot of it all," mutters Bruckard. "Go on then, name your terms."

The beast holds out the manacles. "None of these," it says, dropping them to the floor.

"Fine. What else?"

"Allow me a final revelation."

"When?"

"At this moment. I can bear your ignorance no longer."

"We let you say your final piece, and then you'll go willingly?" Incredulity creeps into Bruckard's voice.

The skeleton places itself between the door and the beast. "By HER will, you will not escape this fate," it promises.

Nodding, the beast says, "I agree to the terms." Its tone is mocking, as if it finds the whole concept of terms and promises beneath it, yet it holds out its open palms in a sign of submission.

The knight will take what he can get. "Let's have it then."

With that, the beast gazes into the eyes of the man, and hell's embers alight within his black pupils. Bruckard tenses, fearing trickery, and then sharply inhales as he bears witness to cold truth. Within the embers, he sees the ruin of the world, the seas blackening, the withering of the vine and the root, the sky weeping flame and stone. He sees men, women, and children pleading for escape, and then for mercy, and then a swift end, and finally for the blessed touch of Yetsabu-Nech, the nightmare. He sees the black-spired city and the marble white throne. He sees a black ship and a beached leviathan upon the ice packed Kergün shores.

Finally, he sees two-legged wolves set loose upon the court, sharing in the blood-cup of the Lady. The largest of the wolves looms large, consuming his field of vision. Horns spring from its head, and its visage twists into the goat-head of That-Which-Bleats. Its black fur begins to shed and an underskin of deepest crimson is revealed. In the beast's right hand is the Gull-Rod of the North, and in its left is the emptied cup of the Lady, and behind it burns the throne.

Behold, says the beast into the knight's mind, *behold your doom and damnation. You are the dog-bitch that will draw the carnal wolves to thy den. Behold your journey's end and the Last Day's beginning. It is wrought, not by great wyrms, nor by maddened queens, nor by the hands of evil men or the nature of beasts . . . nay. It is formed by thy own hand.*

Bruckard tears his eyes away, averting his gaze and crying out, "Nay! It will not!" He casts aside his spear. "Begone, beast, for I will not bring upon this ruin!"

From behind him, he hears the echo of the black mass within the skull, but the words are nigh unfamiliar. Only once has he heard such a sound. It had poured from the mouth of the royal guard before he stumbled in the recitation and the dread power took him.

Now those words are spoken anew, and the skull has no tongue for them to stumble upon. The last line of the spell is spoken clearly. *"Låt den falska gryningen bryta himlen!"*

Bruckard turns and sees the scroll grasped in bony hands. Sees the pack spilled open. Sees fate's promise, and the deception from the second head of SHE, in the burning eye-sockets of his once companion.

Then a blinding flash blasts forth from the scroll, scorching Bruckard's own eyes and searing away his gaze for the rest of his unfortunate life.

From the newly eternal darkness, a weight slams into his chest, knocking him back and prone. A shriek and a wail pour from the beast.

More archaic commands spew from the skeleton. The fabric of the world is twisted and near rent.

Bruckard rolls to the side, reaching blindly for his spear, finding naught but the iron of the discarded manacles. At the sound of a heavy blow above him, he instinctively covers his face. A fur-covered form lands hard atop him. It struggles, attempting to rise, before a second blow descends, striking with a wet crunch. At that, the beast goes limp, its weight pressing him immobile.

Still, he struggles, pressing against it.

Bone clicks against ice as the skeleton raised by SHE moves to stand over him. The polished wood of a crossbow stock presses against his temple, as if lining up the coming blow.

The echo speaks again.

"Face your fate, knight. Our Lady is waiting."

And SHE will not be denied.

A MOSS LIKE WET ASHES

NATE SOUTHARD

THE HOUND'S SKIN had begun to split long ago, bloated flesh ripping to release a terrible odor, but still it remained by her side. Karva leaned down to stroke its patchy, mange-ridden fur, scratching behind the hole that once was an ear.

"Good," she told the dog. It whined in response, an oddly hollow sound.

They stood at the forest's edge. Above, clouds the color of sadness choked the sky. Cold mud sucked at Karva's ankles. A single, horrible shiver ran through her as she peered at the blackened trees, their shadows hanging blacker still. She wrapped her cloak tighter, its decayed smell a strange comfort. The bundle slung over her shoulder threatened to slip loose, but she wrestled it back into place.

No part of her wanted what came next, yet all parts needed it. All other options had vanished. Only the terrible burden before her remained.

Karva swallowed. It felt like a stone in her throat.

"All right," she said. A howl of wind almost swallowed her voice. "Let's go."

The hound gave a short, empty growl in response, and together they crossed the forest's threshold.

Gray and blue shadows devoured the world, and Karva strained to see what waited before her. Tangled, charred tree roots crossed the ground, the forest floor beneath wet with old leaves and mud. The hound crept forward, tried to pant. It snuffled at the ground, and Karva wondered what the dead thing might smell. Over the previous years, she'd grown so accustomed to the death stink that she often thought she could smell nothing else. Were she to wash, would she miss it? Most likely, and that filled her with a queer sadness.

"You and I," she said, and the dog looked up at her, something like affection in its milky eyes. Karva nodded deeper into the woods. "Do you have it?" she asked.

Cracking skin peeled back from the dog's teeth, the grin of something that would soon be a skull.

"Take me," she said, and her dead companion bounded past the trees.

Struggling through the choking wilderness, Karva fell more times than she could count, and soon the mud soaked her frayed robes. Cold suffused her to the very core of her bones, and she breathed foggy breaths through teeth that clacked an unsteady staccato. Somehow, she kept the bundle more or less dry, yet every trip and stumble sent a new shiver of panic through her. She had promised herself she would reach her destination with the parcel intact, and she planned to keep that promise.

The hound kept her moving, always a few steps ahead. Waiting and loyal. Watching. Urging her forward with its dead eyes. For so long, it had been her most faithful companion. As she shuffled after it, the hound's rump wagging like a strange apparatus, she recalled her time as a little girl. The hound had been warm then, and its sloppy kisses on her cheek had made her giggle. Even now, she remembered the swelling surge of happiness whenever the dog curled beside her at night. The feeling of safety.

And then she remembered the years when the hound moved more slowly, when it ate its own sick and whined in terrible pain as it watched her with pleading, rheumy eyes. She would hug it and sob into its warm fur, but nothing helped, and one morning the dog simply refused to wake. Mother buried the hound under a heavy stone deep in the woods. It took Korva forever to find it. Took her even longer to wrestle the stone to one side and dig through the earth with nothing but her fingers. By the time she finished, they'd been raw and bleeding, but everything felt better when the dog opened its eyes again.

It had been the first dead thing Karva had brought back. Her mother had cast her out for playing with such awful magics, bolting the door against her screams and pounding fists. The hound had stayed with her, though, and Karva still felt the trade could have been worse. For so many years, the hound had remained by her side. No one could say she was alone in the world.

"That's right," she said, the strange crack in her voice surprising her.

Karva stepped, and her foot came down in mud, slipping sharply to the side. A gasp escaped her, and she shot out both arms, searching for anything that might stop her fall, but there was nothing. Her breath caught, and there was a terrible instant of weightlessness. Then, she crashed into the wet ground once again.

She clenched her teeth, biting back the angry screech that wanted to peal past them. Frustrated breath shuddering free of her lungs, she wiped cold muck from her eyes. They had to be close. She didn't know if she could handle another fall.

Only when she climbed to her feet did she notice the lack of weight on her back. Panicked, she searched the shadows. The bundle lay a few feet away, coated in filth and half-sunk in a puddle.

"No!" Karva scurried to the bundle and fell to her knees.

With cold, unfeeling hands, she started brushing away what she could. The mud only smeared, further soaking the sodden bundle.

"No, no, no." She held the bundle tight and fought to keep the anguished whine from pouring out of her throat.

Would it all still work? Had this ruined everything? She didn't know, and she wouldn't know until they reached the circle and she tried, but every minor issue only added up to something larger, something worse, and maybe soon everything would have fallen apart.

A sob clucked free of her chest, and tears blurred her eyes. The hound approached with cautious steps and nestled in beside her, but it didn't help. The dog wasn't warm anymore, and she was no longer a little girl. Now, she was so much more, and yet she still felt like nothing at all.

Her tears dried on her cheeks before the hound led her through the clearing's border to the circle of stones. It *was* real, not merely a myth.

Something not unlike a smile threatened to appear, but she chased it away. She still didn't know for sure. Not yet.

The dog padded back and forth at her feet. It whimpered and turned its head toward the circle's center. There, Karva saw a flat, circular stone like a table, like an altar. Gray moss covered its surface. Strange moss like the ashes of a funeral pyre after heavy rains, sopping and thick. Karva's gaze narrowed as the stone called to her, and she felt a low thrumming through her body, a sensation that chased away the cold and filled her with eager anticipation.

She realized she'd been holding her breath. Air eased from her lungs, heavy and cold. She clenched her hands, trying to will feeling back into her numb fingers.

"Do this," she told herself. "Go ahead."

But her feet refused to move. Rooted to the spot, she could only eye the flat stone and its moss. Slowly, she realized the weighted feeling of fear as it settled over her. She knew why. For so long, she'd invested all her hopes in this rock altar and the circle of stones around it. Now and then, she had been able to tell herself it might not be real, that perhaps it was nothing more than a tale told around campfires and whispered in alleyways.

But it was real, and she could no longer deny the truth. It was right in front of her, and that meant she would soon learn if she could truly harness its magic. And, if not? If she failed, the last of her hope would evaporate and disappear. What would she have left then? Pain. Only pain.

The hound pressed against her legs, and the feeling dragged Karva back to her senses. Again, she eyed the circle of stones, only this time she stepped forward, easing the bundle off her shoulder.

A strange warmth rushed through her as she crossed the circle's borders. Something that crackled across her skin and burned roiling in her very center. With each step, it grew hotter. Karva struggled for breath. The air felt like smoke, like the center of an impossible inferno. Sweat rolled into her eyes, and she clamped them shut as she took another step. Her knee buckled, and she almost fell, stumbling but keeping her feet beneath her.

"Please," she said through bared teeth, but she couldn't hear the word. A buzzing filled her ears, a nest of angry hornets that had taken up residence in the center of her skull.

Something snagged her ankle, everything stopping at once, and there was no saving herself this time.

She crashed to the ground, her chin slamming into a stone, and stars erupted behind her eyes. The world swam around her, everything spinning, and at first she didn't notice the hands. Sharp and cold, they erupted from the soft earth and took hold of her wrists, her legs. Decayed flesh hung in tatters off bone. Impossibly strong fingers pinned Karva to the ground. She tried to scream, and rotten digits pushed past her teeth to claw at her tongue.

And then the hound charged into the circle. Braying its hollow noises, it tore into the hand at Karva's mouth. Bones splintered and knuckles cracked, and the dead grip fell way. The dog wasted no time, tearing at the other hands. Karva twisted and yanked, fighting as best she could. Nails ripped at the flesh of her arm, but she bit back her cries. Instead, she tore free and fought her way to her feet.

She saw dozens of them reaching from the soil, scratching and searching. The hound attacked any that came too close. The hands tried to overwhelm it, but it could not be stopped. Frenzied and powerful, it destroyed everything it could reach with its teeth.

She shifted the bundle and returned to the task at hand. A few more steps, and she found herself standing over the flat stone. That strange, gray moss. A swell of dizziness washed over her, and she bit down hard on her lip. The pain brought her back.

With trembling hands, she placed the bundle on the stone. The sopping cloth pulled as she unwrapped it piece by piece. Halfway through, the smell hit her, rotten and cloying. The death stink she'd grown so used to since she'd been cast out, cast aside. It called to her, empowered her. It stilled her hands as she unraveled the last few folds. Then, she stood back and admired her work.

What remained of the woman's head faced her, silent and empty. The eyes had gone, and the lips had blackened and pulled back from yellowed teeth. Most of the hair had fallen out; what was left was wispy and dirty and ragged. One cheekbone shone through split flesh.

Karva's gaze bored into those empty sockets. A blackness like shadow and coal stared back. Perhaps it was empty entirely. How many years had passed? Could any of the soul remain? Would the circle's magic even work? Never before had she tried to bring back something so impossibly dead, but never before had she tried to harness something so arcane. Maybe her power, amplified by the stones, would be enough. Maybe she would get what she craved.

She clasped her hands before her and closed her eyes. Her lips moved, syllables she could hardly comprehend slithering over her tongue. The stones around her trembled, and she felt something black and awful roil in the pit of her belly, a terrible bile that threatened to erupt from her very center. Cold breath kissed her neck, and ghostly fingers danced up her spine. A strength Karva had grown to recognize as the very engine of her magic surged through her. The world quaked and gasped, a miniscule thing that shivered before her.

And then she opened her eyes.

The head stared back at her. Slowly, its desiccated lips began to move. A voice like stale air crept forth.

"Karva," it said.

The bile reached the top of Karva's throat. Tears blurred her vision, but she refused to look away. She would not give it the satisfaction. Her hands jerked into fists, still so like the small fists that had pounded on a door as she begged to be let back inside.

She swallowed and then spoke.

"Mother," she said. "I want you to say you're sorry."

HAGFISH DINNER

IAN SERVAAS

THE HAGFISH WRITHED across the chopping block, pathetically knotting and unknotting itself, weeping gouts of mucus from its corpse-gray skin. Its jawless mouth chewed the air, gurgling a voiceless mewl. Pathetic. Even after the cleaver sent its head rolling across the table, it still pantomimed a plea for help. *Pathetic.*

He loathed these creatures. The pail at his feet squirmed with them, their forms barely visible beneath the rising tide of milky slime, large snot bubbles breaking the surface as they dumbly fought and fucked each other. One by one, their heads joined the growing pile.

The skins came next. His father had shown him a special trick using a pole studded with fish hooks to snare the baggy, worm-like skin. Even in death, the hagfish still pumped out welters of slime. *Why?* Why maintain a vestigial instinct? Nothing ate the hagfish in Onda—there was nothing left *to* eat it.

Carefully slipping the wafer-thin flaying knife under the skin, and peeling the hagfish like a diseased fruit, he thought of all the other fish that used to swim in the lake. Oh, the stories he'd heard of the mustachioed sturgeon, placid rockfish, dazzling goldscales, and even the grotesque goblin fish!

His father had shared the stories he learned upon *his*

father's knee, of men coming home with nets full of fish, traps full of mischievous creatures called "crabs," and even the occasional waterfowl. He wondered how they must have tasted—did their flavors vary as much as their appearances? Did the color of their scales give them different tastes?

His reverie was cut short as the fileting knife carried through into his knuckles. Looking at the shallow wound, he grimly mused that even his blood was tastier than these damn hagfish. The thought of their greasy, snotty flesh revolted him. His wife ran out of creative cooking methods long ago, and their stash of spices dried up years ago. Even the precious pot of salt was on its last few spoonfuls. *Pathetic!*

He skinned the rest of the hagfish, plopping the meat into a brining pot to draw out the slime. From the long shadows cast from the door frame, he knew his wife was already waiting to take her turn in this daily cycle, always with that damn smile. The smile that lied things would get better, that she and their son were grateful for any supper at all.

They all hated hagfish, but it was all they had.

After dinner, while their son played noisily with wooden soldiers whittled from a bottomed out boat, the man retreated outside into the dark. The lake grass he left curing all day should have dried just enough to crumble and pack into his pipe.

The pipe's long, thin stem was the snout of a reed fish. He would have never known what it looked like if not for the crude image scrimshawed across the bowl. It was a glorious pipe and the only thing that brought him much joy, a lucky catch with a trawling net. It made a cheery, satisfactory gurgle-chirp as he nursed the blossoming cherry. The acrid, grassy tang of lake grass always cut the hagfish-film on his tongue. It was a luxury worth the lingering cough he'd developed.

Overhead, the miasmic sky became more tolerable as

its sepulcher gray haze melted into the dark. When the wind blew just right and tugged at the perpetual cloud cover, the stars would wink through. He puffed. The stars were different when he was a kid, he thought, back before the sky was poisoned. Somehow, they seemed more numerous, as if scads of them withered and died, but that there were any stars still up there was enough for him.

He could never put a finger on when it happened, when the world entered its death rattles, if there was a certain day or a gradual decay unnoticed until far too late. The red-robed priests in the city cried that the calendar was racing towards the final days. *Bah!* He puffed again. Fuck the priests. They claimed that Basilisks whispered the truth to them, but it was impossible to know the end or the beginning of such things. The world was dying and it was pointless to piss and moan about it, and even worse to philosophize about it.

He sucked in a mouthful of smoke and chewed on it, stewing. *Fuck priests*! What good was knowing things were only going to get worse? Can't do shit about it anyways. It's all fucking hagfish dinners forever. He started to say, *"Maybe it would be better if the world just hurried up and died already,"* but thought of his son and choked on his puff. A father's job is to make things better, even when they're at their worst. That's what his father did, anyway. He sighed and the pipe went out.

As he dumped the bowl and flicked ash from his trousers, the lights darkened in the house and the shutters closed. *Might as well pack another*, he shrugged. It was better to sneak in after his wife fell asleep and save both of them the embarrassment of feigning love around their son.

Repacked, he slurped on the pipe sending a burble of smoke into the air. "*A father's job . . .* " His shame rose with the trailing smoke. He should have left with the others to find work in the city. Hell, even being a gong-farmer would be better than this, but he just couldn't leave the lake. It was in his blood; generations of his family lived and died on this very shore. It was supposed to get better; it was *always* supposed to get better. A promise that ruined a lifetime. Ruined generations.

And he was the last. All around him were the empty houses from people who'd given up and walked away. Most of the homes sagged, silently decaying under the elements, their vacant windows like eye sockets of skulls staring blindly across the lake. He sat until the ember withered in his pipe, then took one final, sooty drag of smoke, pulling the ash deep into his lungs and launching a violent coughing fit.

The sky churned and roiled above him, the chaos reflecting across the placid surface of the lake. When the stars faded and no longer shone through the tortured firmament, he trudged to bed for another night of dreamless, uneasy sleep.

However, against all odds, he *did* dream. He dreamt of the cold waters of the lake, like freezing ink. It was a sea of black like the void of space, and he was a fish lost in those dark fathoms. He swam over rocks, between dead branches, and always found himself alone. He swam through ancient shipwrecks, boats torn apart by war, boats sunk from fishing accidents, the countless sunken graves of men's folly. And yet, he could not find another living thing, not a snail, not a frog, not even a hagfish. The feeling of isolation weighed heavily upon him, pulling him down like a great anchor. A vast emptiness stretched out before his unblinking eyes. He was truly alone.

Yet, there *was* something there in the darkness. He could feel himself being watched, even though he couldn't tell from where. Swimming in circles, he looked all around him, seeing nothing but shadows cast in blackness. Something knew he was there; the sensation intensified, boring into his scales, skewering him like a hook and reeling him down, deep down, into the deepest depths of the lake.

It pulled him so far into the abyss that the weight of

water began crushing him. Bones snapped in his tail and his gills slammed shut, and the force pulled him deeper still. Fear gripped him; he knew he was utterly powerless against this force. He desperately looked up for a glimpse of the surface, but everything was stygian black. He felt like he was trapped in an endless current pulling him towards the gullet of something ancient and hungry and terrible.

After what seemed an eternity, his descent ended. The bottom of the lake rushed up to meet him; it was carpeted with the bones of all the fish that tried to flee this place and failed. With the impact of a plunging boulder, his ichthyoid form was dashed upon the countless others who died here, their bones skewering him like spears.

The next day, his cough was worse. He went about his daytime chores, but at the back of his mind, the dream lingered: the dark waters, the loneliness, the field of bones. It was late afternoon by the time he headed out to fish for dinner. The clouds darkening the horizon warned him of an incoming storm, so he had to make haste. He walked along the shoreline by his house, setting out his lines knowing he would catch nothing; an exercise of futility that was ritual at this point. He shoved out in his small rowboat and threw out his trawl line, dragging it towards the deeper spots where the hagfish lurked. The sky overhead was ash gray, an unending sea of churning, roiling clouds. Lake Onda reflected the dreary expanse across her surface. *As above, so below* he thought.

A disturbance in the water caught his eye. He was surprised to see a hagfish spitting gouts and plumes of slime, furiously knotting and unknotting, as if desperately trying to escape a predator. A curious thing, as there were no predators anymore, besides himself and his lines bobbing idly at the shoreline. Rowing closer, he peered down to see what troubled the fish. Deep scores ran along its slippery skin and it writhed in agony. The end of its tail was snared under an oddly pitted stone.

He pulled a spare rod and dropped a line to pull the

stone up and let the fish go. No point in letting it scare off the others; with their noxious slime, hagfish had a way of knowing when other hagfish were distressed. The hook snagged the stone and the rod groaned with the strain as he lifted. The hagfish squirmed free, sending out a few more plumes of snot before darting away, into the inky recess of the lake's inner depths. The stone remained stuck fast on his line, no matter how much he shook it. Not wanting to waste line nor rod, he did the only sensible thing and carefully reeled it in.

As it crested the waters, he realized it wasn't a stone, but a skull, clearly human, mottled and stained with the detritus swirling at the lake's bottom for countless years. Patches of lake grass clung to it like clumps of hair. It leered at him with empty sockets lined by grime and the shells of long dead mollusks. He carefully pried loose the hook and untangled the line caught in its teeth. Cradling it in his hands, he contemplated it. He had seen all kinds of shipwrecks, signs of war and death, and occasional bones, but never any *skulls.* It seemed odd, portentous even. He set it down and debated whether he should bury the skull as a sign of respect, or perhaps toss it back like the flotsam it was.

A peal of thunder in the distance heralded the coming storm. The skull would have to wait. He set about casting a new net and prayed that the hagfish wouldn't be scared off.

"*They can't hear you,*" a voice whispered. "*Your gods are dead. Their thrones sit empty.*"

No one was near, nor any other boats on the water. He took a sip of water from an old canteen and swallowed down his nerves, telling himself he must have been imagining things, the countless parade of so many sleepless nights toying with his mind.

The sky above churned black and more thunder rolled over the yawning hills. He fussed with a persistent knot that threatened to foul the whole net. As he struggled, something flashed in the water and he leaned over to look. It was a riot of fish, all the fish from his boyhood stories! He saw a goblin fish munching on a school of sliver-like darkfins while goldscales darted past, their metallic bodies reflecting aquatic rainbows in their wake. A majestic herald trout crested the surface, saluting the sky with its standard-like snout before diving back under. All the while, a walleyed Fathmu fish glowered disapprovingly, wrinkling its thick, golden brow at the others.

His excitement and bewilderment rose in equal spades. Scrabbling at the knot, he ripped it free and tossed out the net as fast as he could. As it sank and the waters settled, the lake was empty once again. All of the fish had vanished. He peered feverishly in all directions, trying to catch a glimpse of something, anything flitting away, but saw nothing. He sat down, put his head between his knees, and rubbed his eyes. Surely, he was going crazy.

The daylight dwindled in the dark of the approaching storm. Lightning danced across its underbelly like the light across phantom fish. He prayed aloud, asking for a pair of hagfish so at least his wife and son could eat. A laughter of dry rolling leaves tumbled through the air.

"*You pray to dead gods . . . for* hagfish? *Pathetic.*"

He turned, and met the empty eye sockets of the skull boring into his.

"*The lake used to teem with all manner of fish,*" it went on.

"*Not just fish, but eels, turtles, crabs, shrimp, all manner of things just begging to be snared by hook and net.*"

He gaped in terror, his mouth opening and closing like a beached fish, unable to express his surprise. The storm rumbled in the distance, as if speaking for him

"*I have seen much from the bottom; the dying of the sky, the lake stealing away its gifts, the stubborn decay of the village. And . . . you.*" Something in the skull's countenance seemed to suggest it was furrowing a brow that rotted along ago. "*You are still here, refusing to leave. Why?*"

The man continued to gape dumbly at first, but a drop of cold rain splashed his face and snapped him back to focus. He swallowed. "Because . . . there is nowhere else to go."

The skull grinned. *"But, that's not* really *why, is it? No, you've told yourself a lie to cling onto like a drowning man clings to driftwood."*

Its accusation punctured the thick air. He felt like a fish on a hook.

"It's because I believed the stories. That the lake would return its gifts to the faithful, that we would never go hungry." The grin seemed to broaden.

"And? How full is your net today?" it chided. *"How has your faith been rewarded?"*

He didn't need to reel in the net to know it was still empty. Across the lake, his pole-lines were slack. A cold wind rippled across the lake, and petrichor followed in its wake. Dazzling ropes of lightning were chased by roaring thunder. The distant light of his hovel flickered like a tiny candle in the gloom. It would be impossible to reach before the storm gobbled him up.

Rain plinked off the skull. "*Oh deary me. Looks like rain. Can't have that, now can we? Come on then, I'll show you a place just ahead where we can wait out the storm together*." It grinned again, turning its empty gaze leeward.

The man didn't have time to question; a snap of thunder made his decision and he churned the oars instinctively. The wind increased, shoving waves against the boat, speeding it further from the safe light of home.

"There," rattled the skull, *"over there."*

They were shooting towards an islet. At first, the storm's shadow and sheeting rain made the shape unfamiliar, but as the boat clipped a buoy, recognition gripped him.

"The blighted skerry!" He didn't need light to know

that its craggy shore was encrusted with crimson lichen and bristling with red reeds. It was an ill-omened place, one his father and father's father had warned against trespass. A sudden jolt of lightning illuminated the tilting menhirs that jutted out like broken teeth across its surface.

He slapped his oars to break hard and turn, but an undercurrent clutched the boat and reeled it in.

"That's what you call it? That's a terrible name." The skull gurgled as rainwater poured in through its eye sockets.

The man launched a protest that was swallowed by a tattoo of thunder. Against his wishes, the boat crashed into the shore, making every plank groan and shooting cracks along the hull. He lashed out with a rope and fixed it against a rocky projection, feeling shivers down his spine as his fingers traced deep runes carved by ancient hands.

"Up there, there's shelter," the skull shouted over the keening wind. *"A dolmen."* As the man started up the scraggy slope, it barked, *"Don't forget me, you dolt!"*

He turned, choking down disgust at picking up the talking thing, but did so obediently, cradling it under his arm as he climbed. At the end of the henge squatted a dolmen made of wide slabs of crumbling stone. Somehow, the darkness within seemed even more caliginous than the storming night sky above. In front of its yawning mouth sat what looked to be a low altar, plastered with more of that red lichen resembling dried blood.

"In you git!" The skull bit at his ribs, and he started with a yelp.

Inside, the dolmen was cavernous. The stone seemed to breathe in the storm's rage and exhale silence. It felt like being in the depths of a tomb with only the occasional splash of lightning reminding him of the outside world. They waited motionlessly in the solemn darkness as time trickled slowly. In the quiet, all he could hear was his own heaving breath. The walls smothered him, closing all around him. He felt as if he was entombed alive in a silent grave, powerless to move or speak. It reminded him of his dream, and the helpless terror he felt as a fish.

The silence was cracked by the susurrus of the skull, its tone almost reverent.

"This place is special. Can you feel it?" The quiet settled back in like a pall until he found his tongue and spoke.

"My father warned me of this place." His words seemed far too loud and he lowered them to a hush. "Said devils worshiped here, catching fishermen who wandered too close to shore. The buoys were warnings not to trespass."

"Fools," spat the skull, somehow both as clamant as a thunderclap and quiet as a gloved slap. *"You sit upon sacred soil and enjoy the shelter given by ones more ancient than memory. This was the place where the gods first alighted. Not your 'old gods,' no; gods far more old than that. They left their mark here. It's still here, even after all these years."*

Unease coursed through his veins. He felt wrong. He shouldn't be here; he should have risked floundering to get home.

"Look," the skull instructed.

The man shut his eyes. If you made eye contact with a devil, it'd take you.

"Look," it repeated.

He pressed his eyes so tightly that stars swam out.

"LOOK!" commanded the skull.

His eyes opened. Did he do that? Did it do that? The dark in the back of the dolmen was still absolute, but as his eyes adjusted, he could see the faint outlines of something.

"Yes, look at it."

Fear slithered down his spine like cold snakes, and his pulse quickened.

Outside, the storm quelled, taking with it the sky's obscuring haze. The stars blossomed, providing a rare treat of starlight. The interior lit up with a faint glow, revealing the shape to be just a gnarled and twisted rock. He let out a sigh as he realized his nerves had gotten the best of him.

The skull, still perched in his lap, swiveled and looked up at him. *"This baetylus is the exact spot where the first gods perched upon their creation."* The words hung in the air. *"Your gods are dead, their corpses fouling the Shimmering Fields, but the first ones can never die. They merely* sleep.*"*

"How do you know the old gods are dead?" he asked, his voice marred with sorrow.

The skull replied first with a stare, then softened and paternally cooed, *"You know it to be true deep in your marrow. You know your prayers go unanswered, your faith wasted. You don't need me to confirm your fears. The world is dying all around us. What you want is comfort . . . and purpose."*

Yes, the words stabbed like a honeyed knife. Yes, he wanted to give up the charade, the chore of maintaining the home shrine, and wasting good food upon the family altar.

"The first ones sleep, but they are not deaf. In their dreamless slumber, they yearn for creation to once again sing their praises," the skull continued, its voice reverential. *"They are listening to us even now."*

It felt like the strange stone took on a luster he hadn't observed before. Perhaps it was just the starlight, but a yearning stirred in his heart. Hope . . . he craved *hope.*

Like a petulant child, his stomach rumbled. In the excitement of the day, he had forgotten his hunger. Then guilt stabbed him. What about his family? His wife and child went hungry and must think him lost to the storm. He chose his words carefully, but they still dripped with frustration. "If the first ones are still alive, then why must I suffer? Why do I starve? Why don't they help?"

"The first ones suffer no fools," the skull snarled. *"They were wronged and took back their blessings as punishment."*

The skull let the words hang in the air until the man grasped their meaning.

"The fish. They took the fish!"

The skull nodded approvingly. *"Yes, that is why the lake is barren. Your people abandoned their faith and failed to abide by their promises, so they were punished."*

Somehow he felt guilty, as if the sins of his ancestors weighed solely on his shoulders, and it was *his* fault that his family starved.

Outside, the storm's strength seemed to be waning. The trailing wind cleared patches of the cloud-strewn sky, letting a rare shaft of moonlight slip through. Pale light splashed into the dolmen, and he could see curious runes and faded pictographs across the walls.

"What was their failing?" He traced his eyes along the stone slabs looking for a clue.

"Fear. Fear and weakness." The skull's words were burning coals. *"A wizard, a foul necromancer, clawed its way out from the Valley of Unfortunate Dead, seeking to defile this sacred place in exchange for fell powers."*

The man grew wide-eyed. The necromancer was a boogeyman used to scare children into good behavior or serve as a foil in morality parables. His blood ran cold to think it was real.

The skull continued in a hushed, warding tone. *"Your people abandoned their faith and gave in to fear. They fled and let the blessed islet be fouled, its ancient graves upheaved, the cairns scattered, and the menhirs toppled."* Oddly it paused to grind its teeth and grimace, as if recalling something painful. *"Only one stood against the necromancer, the high priest who dwelled on the islet, and he died an agonizing, miserable death."* The skull trembled as it chewed on its following words. *"Flayed alive, piece by piece, limbs severed and scattered into the lake while the wizard's dark powers kept him alive."*

The man's skin crawled in sympathy and dread. He broke into a cold sweat as the terrible recognition dawned. "You," he gulped. "You were the priest."

A wan smile spread across the skull. *"Aye. I died in this*

very spot, ages upon ages ago. But I never abandoned my faith." It locked its sockets with the man's gaze. *"I knew I would, some day, be found, and I could undo the damage that was wrought here."* Resolutely, with renewed strength, the skull declared, *"I will begin by returning the fish to Onda."*

A cauldron of conflicting emotions burbled within him, but the prospect of fish again sent hope spilling out. Visions of plenty dazzled in his mind and the spectacle from before replayed over and over. His reverie was interrupted by the clacking of teeth.

"To do this, I require your help." Its voice swelled, filling the dolmen with a sonorous charge. *"You must recover my bones. Rebuild me and you shall be rewarded."*

The man nodded with excitement and affirmation.

"For now, leave me to my prayers. Return home to your family. We will begin tomorrow."

He shot up like a bolt, nearly hitting his head on the low ceiling, and stumbled out into the night. In his boat, along with several inches of water, were a pair of hagfish.

His wife was asleep, draped over the open window, having fallen asleep during her vigil. Their son was curled up by her feet, clutching his wooden soldiers tightly. Looking upon them, he felt love—genuine love—swell in his haggard heart. He woke them with an embrace.

A father's job is to make things better.

And he was going to do that.

The next day, he returned to the islet and found the skull exactly where he left it. In the paltry daylight, it looked cleaner and less aged somehow, as if it got a good night's sleep too.

"*Let us begin. We have much to do.*"

Propped in the bow of his boat, the skull directed the man where to pilot and where to drop lines. The first day was the most grueling. He had never rowed even half the length of Onda in a day before, yet, by sunfall he had crossed nearly the whole length, dredging the shallows and scraping deep mudflats with a muckrake. The entire day's labor offered only a fistful of vertebrae, knuckle bones, and other smaller bones. But the man's spirits were buoyed by the thought of a real fish dinner, and he never complained.

The following days became more fruitful as they probed the deeper parts of the lake. Over a single afternoon, they fished an entire leg and foot's worth of bones, which brought glee to both the skull and man. On another day, they discovered a knot of hagfish that had lined their nest with snot and broken ribs; the hagfish fled at the sight of the skull, as if they knew their trophies were stolen.

Days turned into weeks, and weeks into a full month, but the man never tired. As they hunted for the missing bones, the skull taught him all about the world's ancient history, stories of the first ones, and, of course, everything about the fish he could expect. As much as he wanted to learn the *true* faith of his people, it was the fish he couldn't stop thinking about. Thunder carp swam through the sulci of his brain and shoals of gray-swifts darted through his thoughts. His mouth watered involuntarily and he imagined the taste of each one, and what their flesh would smell like roasting over an open spit. He imagined more flesh on his wife's willowy form and strong muscles on his growing son as they grew fat on a feast of fish.

The last bones were the most difficult. The skull steered him to the center of the lake where it was deepest.

"There. Down there are the last pieces of me."

It was far too deep for the man to dive, so he fashioned a system of weighted buckets with trapped air to help him reach the bottom. As he descended into the crushing darkness, fear shooed the imaginary bounties of fish from his mind and creeped in with cold talons. His chest tightened and he struggled to breathe. He wanted to panic but heard a hissing admonishment from the skull in his mind, *"fear and weakness."* He would show neither. He was faithful, faithful to the true gods and was on a course of redemption.

The bottom was littered with fishbones, just like in his dream. *Coincidence*, he thought, denying the tendrils of fear fishing for purchase again. He combed through the bone carpet, plucking out the final missing pieces. On the way up, he thought he saw something else lingering in the aquatic graveyard, but didn't have the air to spare a second glance. When he hauled himself into the boat, lungs burning and coughing up gouts of lake water, the skull smiled warmly.

"You have done well. So very well. We are almost at the end."

They returned to the islet a final time and the man laid down the final bones into the skeleton stretched across the altar.

"Complete me and let me reward your faith."

The air crackled with anticipation as the man picked up the grinning skull and nestled it into its spine. The stench of ozone rose from the slab, accompanied by an assortment of clicks, snaps, and grinding scrapes. Piece by piece, each bone linked together like bricks being set into place. The skull moaned painfully, yet almost in ecstasy. Fine sinew sprouted from joints like weeds between rocks, lashing bones together with fleshy tendrils.

The man watched in rapt fascination and horror as the skull was covered with unfurling strips of milky-white tendons and blood vessels snaked across its surface. The moan became a wet, gurgling wheeze, and then a cackling laugh of triumph. With the creaking of a dying tree, the skull, itself now a fully-formed skeleton, rose from the altar, arms outstretched. Tiny pin-pricks of red light danced in the skeleton's dark eye sockets. Its jaw, clattering unevenly as tendons stretched and retracted, uttered the words: *"TIME FOR YOUR REWARD."*

The skeleton lunged, its sharp, bony fingers puncturing the man's skin, parting it like a knife through hagfish skin.

The man screamed louder than he thought possible as he tried to pull away, but the bony fingers dug through his meat and gripped his bones, holding him fast. With practiced ease, the skeleton moved its hands under the man's skin, being careful to not nick any vital blood vessels, letting the agony go on and on. The man struggled feebly and wetly as pain stole his strength, but the skeleton calmly continued its work unhindered.

His skin was plopped piece by piece into a wet pile until all his innards were exposed to the air. Then the skeleton let go, sending the man tumbling to the ground. Gasping and floundering, his mouth mutely chewed the air, making a silent mewl of agony. He felt an unbearable cold sink into his burning nerves and he convulsed violently, spewing bloody phlegm across himself. The skeleton was already slipping into his harvested skin, the pieces stitching themselves together with sickly tendrils.

The last thing the man saw with his bulging, wide eyes was his own face staring back. Sharp, fierce eyes judged him. *"Pathetic."* The necromancer turned and walked away, down the islet, into the lake, and out again, heading westward until it faded into the horizon. The lake, no longer fouled, sighed as the fish returned, filling the waters with a riot of life.

ECHOES OF ETERNITY

ZACK ALLEN

FUCK, IT WAS FREEZING. The bitter chill clawed at him relentlessly, gnawing at his bones with icy fangs; each exhale materializing into ghostly clouds that created a haunting dance in the frigid air. The jagged terrain, strewn with cruel stones, tore at his flesh, unleashing a river of agony as his feet wept blood and pus, painting the earth in a grotesque tableau of suffering.

Traversing the treacherous slopes, he moved with an almost robotic deliberation, his descent hindered not only by the cruel geography but also by the enigmatic fog that clouded his mind. Memories, once vivid, now lay shrouded in a thick mist of uncertainty, leaving him adrift in a sea of confusion. Yet amidst the oppressive cold and the looming shadows of the landscape, one thought persisted: the primal instinct to return home, to seek solace in the warmth of familiarity. But home remained but a distant dream, obscured by the relentless tempest that swept through the desolate wastes before him. The landscape, a canvas of desolation, offered no respite, its unforgiving terrain a testament to nature's indifference to human suffering; and still, the questions lingered like a specter on the wind: how, and why, had he come to this accursed place?

His reflection, a mockery of his former self, stared back at him from the murky depths of his mind. Hollow eyes, framed by wisps of white hair and pallid skin weathered by the relentless passage of time, bore witness to the toll exacted by his harrowing journey. Each step forward felt like a battle against oblivion, a desperate struggle against the encroaching darkness that threatened to consume him whole. Yet, amidst the bleakness of his plight, a glimmer of clarity pierced the veil of confusion. Memories, long buried beneath layers of forgotten time, began to resurface, fragments of a past lost to the abyss. How long had he wandered these desolate wastes? The answer eluded him, a tantalizing enigma that whispered of secrets yet to be revealed. In the shadowed recesses of his mind, he clawed his way back to awareness, the tendrils of fog slowly receding like the tide revealing jagged rocks beneath. It was a precarious awakening, akin to emerging from the depths of a nightmare only to find the nightmare had followed him into the waking world. His faculties, once shrouded in darkness, now flickered with a feeble light, weakly illuminating the desolation that surrounded him. He had only just begun to scratch the surface of this twisted new reality, to peel back the layers of madness and despair that cloaked it like a mourner's veil, when panic began to grip him with a chill far deeper than any wind could muster. How long had he drifted through his own life, buffeted by unseen currents of cosmic influence? Days? Weeks? Perhaps longer? The passage of time had become a twisted enigma–a riddle whispered by unseen specters in the haunted halls of his mind.

The gravelly terrain clawed at his worn soles, etching a painful gash across an already blistered foot. Agony surged through his veins like a malevolent current, jolting him to a sudden halt. Refusing to confront the grisly sight of blood pooling beneath him, he clenched his jaw against the impending tears, his face contorting in a futile battle against the onslaught of emotion. When he finally mustered the courage to glance downward, the facade of stoicism shattered like glass. Tears, hot and unrelenting, streaked down his weathered cheeks, carving clean paths through the grime like rivulets etching stone. Collapsing into a fetal crouch, he folded himself tightly, rocking back and forth in the chill embrace of the dry, biting wind, his sobs swallowed by the churning desolation surrounding him.

As the tears dried and the sobs waned, he remained seated, his spirit pleading for the strength to persevere, his cries echoing into the uncaring void. Casting his gaze across the bleak expanse that held him captive, he beheld a landscape steeped in sorrow and dread. He mused on his possible whereabouts, finding little solace in the prospect of either fate; yet, trapped in this desolate realm, he would sooner brave the clutches of the Blood Countess herself than endure the desolation of this forsaken wasteland. With each passing moment, the truth of his location became more undeniable. Bergen Chrypt loomed before him, a name whispered in hushed tones, a place where darkness reigned supreme. Its origins shrouded in mystery, the land now lay in ruin, a testament to the cruelty of time and the malevolence of the forces that dwell within. Rumored to have once been a land of great magnificence, now reduced to a barren expanse of shattered peaks and jagged cliffs, it harbors unspeakable horrors and vile creatures spawned from the depths of nightmare. Shaking off his reverie, he forced himself to focus on his surroundings, though every fiber of his being recoiled from the prospect. Despite his efforts, the landscape offered no reprieve, no sign of life amidst the desolation. If there were people living here, they remained elusive, concealed within the shadows of this forsaken realm. Now, knowing where he stood, he questioned whether he truly wished to uncover the secrets buried within the heart of Bergen Chrypt.

He rose from the desolation, a man driven by despair and the shadows that danced in his mind. In the gloom of the forsaken landscape, he scoured for a tool, a shard of stone sharp enough to cut the tether of his existence. The first rock he gripped offered only a blunt resistance against his skin, a mocking reminder of his futile attempts to escape the grip of despair. But he persisted, driven by an inner torment that gnawed at his soul. In the depths of his desperation, he made a grim pact with himself. If death was to claim him, it would be on his own terms, not at the whim of some ravenous abomination lurking in the shadows. With a grim determination, he ventured forth, his footsteps echoing against the desolate cliffs as he sought his deliverance. Then, as if summoned from the depths of his darkest nightmares, he beheld a sight that defied reason. A town, nestled within the jagged embrace of the valley below–a beacon of hope amidst the surrounding wasteland. His resolve wavered as newfound hope coursed through his veins, banishing thoughts of death from his mind. But fate, it seemed, had other plans. As he staggered towards the promise of salvation, the sky itself rebelled, unleashing a tempest of unparalleled fury upon the unsuspecting town below. The air crackled with the fury of a vengeful god, and he watched in horror as the very fabric of reality unraveled before his eyes. In that moment all hope was lost. The twister, a maelstrom of chaos and destruction, erupted through the valley with merciless intent, consuming everything in its path. Starring in silent terror and disbelief he fell, almost gently, to his knees, his spirit shattered by the cruel twist of fate; and as the storm bore down upon him, he closed his eyes, resigned to his fate. With a savage force the wind hurled him aside, casting him to the ground and driving his temple into a large stone; and as darkness claimed him, he could feel that his journey had only just begun.

In the midst of the pending twilight, shadows danced around the ramshackle homestead, keeping hidden the secrets of long-forgotten repairs. She stood there, her voice like honey dripping from a darkened hive, her silhouette against the fading light a portrait of domesticity tinged with the unknown.

“What do ye want fer supper?”

“Supper?” The word hung in the air like a promise unfulfilled, a question that held more weight than it should. What did he want for supper? The answer eluded him, lost in the shadows of his own mind.

“Oh, I dunno,” he murmured, drawing on his pipe; the words slipping from his lips like the smoke tendrils twining between his yellowed teeth. His gaze wandered, drawn to the expanse of their land, a patchwork of shadows and secrets that stretched to the edge of Galgen Woods. The scent of spring hung heavy in the air, mingling with the metallic tang of blood and the earthy musk of decay. It was a tableau of contradiction, where beauty danced hand in hand with the grotesque. He watched as the bees flitted about, oblivious to the impending darkness that threatened to swallow them whole. Perhaps a stew, he mused, a concoction of leftover meat and mystery simmering over the hearth. She did make a fine stew. Yet, the thought of boar turned his stomach, a reminder of hunts past and sins unforgiven. As if summoned by his thoughts, a creature emerged from the brush nearby–a jackalope, a creature of myth and madness. A third eye adorning its face stared back at him, offering a window to a realm beyond comprehension.

“I was thinkin’ a nice pie with boar and vegetables,” she continued, her voice laced with undertones of annoyance at his indecision. But his attention had been stolen by the creature before him, its gaze piercing through the veil of reality. A cacophony of sound assaulted his senses, a symphony of madness conducted by unseen hands. Amidst the chaos, a voice emerged; a whisper inside his own head that cut through the din like a knife.

"Hello there, I was just admiring the bees. Do you want to be friends?" It spoke not with the warmth of the living, but with the cold detachment of the dead. His ears rang with the echo of its words, drowning out the whirlwind of madness assaulting his mind. Beside him, his wife remained oblivious, lost in her own world of domestic musings; but he couldn't shake the feeling that something was terribly wrong, that the world around him was unraveling at the seams.

"It has been so long since I have found someone nice to talk to," the voice purred flatly. "I see you like the bees, as I do. Would you come along?" His mind reeled, struggling to comprehend the absurdity of the situation. Yet, despite his disbelief, his body betrayed him, inching slowly towards the source of the otherworldly voice.

"You won't?" The voice persisted, its tone dripping with a feigned sadness. "Oh, how I long to talk with one who could calm my curiosity and be a friend. Won't you please come with me?" With each step towards the Jackalope, his sense of unease deepened, gnawing at the edges of his sanity. His thoughts swirled in a maelstrom of confusion and fear, unable to grasp the reality of what was unfolding before him.

"I am not impossible," the voice assured him, as if reading his thoughts, though it did little to quell his rising dread. "And soon we will be able to talk for as long as we want, about everything. No more questions. Come, now." As he drew closer, the forest seemed to pulse with a malevolent energy, its ancient trees whispering secrets of unspeakable horror. In a desperate attempt to reassert his grasp on reality he glanced back at his wife, only to recoil in horror at the grotesque mockery of humanity that stood before him. Her form, twisted and contorted, bore little resemblance to the woman he once knew. Blood-red stains marred her skin, her eyes glinting with an otherworldly hunger. A wicked grin stretched across her face, revealing rows of razor-sharp teeth that glistened in the dim light. The air grew thick with the stench of decay as the abomination that wore his wife's visage beckoned him closer, its unholy maw gaping wide with anticipation. With a sinking heart he realized that he had stumbled into a nightmare from which there would be no escape, and as the cooing voice called to him from the darkness, he turned and ran headlong into the depths of a madness from which few ever returned.

In the murky recesses of his consciousness, a crimson glimmer flickered, casting a ghastly hue upon the void. There, amidst the undulating shadows, loomed the unyielding gaze of a malevolent entity, its scarlet gleam piercing the darkness, an unyielding stare that seared his soul. He jolted awake, the echo of screams reverberating through his skull. At first, he was certain the screams were his own, but then a chilling realization struck: they were coming from within his mind. As the cacophony ceased, a chill slithered down his spine, for he found himself no longer perched upon the familiar ridge where consciousness had abandoned him. His feet, puppeteered by forces unseen, propelled him downward, into the abyss where the tornado had devoured his last hope of salvation. Yet, where devastation once reigned, now lay only an empty valley, devoid of both catastrophe and civilization. Had it all been a fevered dream? Straining against the unseen forces guiding him, he stumbled to a halt, the abruptness nearly toppling him. Amidst the desolation, a solitary edifice loomed–a spire of unknown purpose, casting ominous shadows in the dimming light. There, in the gloom, stood the three-eyed Jackalope, its presence a harbinger of impending doom.

"Almost there," it cooed, its words dripping with malicious intent. "Just a little farther, then we can converse properly." Was it an invitation, or a veiled threat? Questions swirled within his mind, a tempest of uncertainty. What sinister machinations drove this creature? Why had it lured him here to this forsaken place? With each passing moment, the fabric of reality unraveled before him, revealing glimpses of a spectral masquerade. Phantoms of the long-departed cavorted in a macabre dance, adorned in ancient robes with high collars of hardened silk and strange hats that looked like sensual flowers. Amidst the throng an ethereal couple spun in his direction, the woman dipping back towards him limply like a snake, her grin a grotesque parody of beauty. Her breath, a fetid miasma of decay and infestation, seared his senses, leaving him stunned and trembling. Blinking away tears, he watched as the spectral revelry dissolved into nothingness and he found himself alone once more, save for the Jackalope's watchful gaze amidst encroaching darkness.

In the dim glow of an otherworldly twilight, his words clawed their way out of a throat thick with dread, his voice a rasping echo of his own terror. Each syllable hung heavy in the air, a desperate plea swallowed by the oppressive silence that surrounded him. His sense of time had eroded like the crumbling edges of a forgotten tombstone, leaving only the disorienting void of eternal night. Was it still today? Or had the grasp of madness already ensnared him in its suffocating embrace?

"Whu-wha-what duh-do you wuh-want from muh-muh-me?" His words, a feeble attempt to pierce the shroud of uncertainty that enveloped him, trembled with a resolve born of desperation. Yet, even as he spoke, he knew deep within the marrow of his bones that there would be no solace in the answer. The Jackalope's third eye, a grotesque aberration glistening with the promise of revelations darker than the abyss itself, beckoned him forward with a silent allure. Its insidious pull tugged at the fraying edges of his sanity, drawing him ever closer to the precipice of his own undoing. With each faltering step, he stumbled deeper into the labyrinthine depths of his own fractured psyche, the world around him warping and contorting like the fevered hallucinations of a mind teetering on the brink of oblivion. Yet, even amidst the chaos, a fragment of memory lingered, a haunting specter from a time long forgotten. As he trailed behind the horned harbinger of his own descent, its antlers swaying in macabre cadence to a rhythm only it could hear, he was consumed by the spectral visage of a past that refused to stay buried. It was not the shadowed dancers of Bergen Chrypt that haunted him now, but something far more insidious–an echo of a life lost to the void, and a whisper of horrors yet to come.

In the shifting shadows of twilight the Jackalope's form twisted seamlessly, contorting into that of a black goat perched upon a rickety wagon. The air was thick with the foul stench of rot and urine, a noxious fume that clung to the city like a putrid fog. The odor clawed its way into his nostrils, evoking memories long buried beneath layers of time and regret. Schleswig. The name whispered through his mind like a curse, dredging up visions of past visits, both innocent and tainted by the darkness that now enveloped his soul. With the detachment of a spectator, he watched as the wagon halted before a dilapidated hovel, its weathered facade a testament to the decay festering within. Descending from the wagon, he retrieved an obsidian ocarina, its surface etched with ancient runes of forbidden knowledge. As he played a discordant melody, the air thickened with energy, a prelude to the macabre ritual about to unfold.

A peculiar rhythm echoed from within the shack, a coded summons to which he responded in kind, his pulse quickening with anticipation. The door creaked open, revealing a hideous figure framed in its threshold. The man's features were a grotesque caricature, his lips contorting into a leering grin, and with a predatory gleam in his narrowed eyes, he ushered his guest inside, sealing their fate with a click of the lock. As the repugnant man shed his garments, the air grew heavy with dread, anticipation mingling with primal instinct in a dance of death. With a surge of primal fury, he seized the rat-faced man by the throat, his fingers coiling like serpents around the fragile sinew of his neck. A silent plea flickered in the depths of the man's gaze as life slowly ebbed from his wretched form, his struggles futile against the inexorable grip of death. The man's pupils appeared to spill outward as the last vestiges of consciousness slipped away, leaving only the echo of a final gasp. With trembling hands, he rummaged through the remains of the dead man, his fingers questing for the prize hidden amidst the mundane; and there, nestled within the folds of cloth, he found it–a shard of obsidian matching that of the ocarina, a fragment of forbidden truth pulsating with otherworldly power. With a surge of madness, he drove the shard into his skull, its razor edge tearing through flesh and bone with a sickening crunch. As darkness swallowed him whole, he welcomed the embrace of oblivion, a willing sacrifice to the eldritch forces that lay beyond the veil of sanity.

As his consciousness slammed back into his body, his hand instinctively reached for his throbbing skull. A sudden surge of pain pinpointed the source–a sharp, glassy protrusion piercing through flesh and bone, nestled just off-center from his receding hairline. How had such an obvious anomaly escaped his notice until now? The fresh pain pulsating from the wound offered little explanation.

"You missed," the Jackalope's voice echoed, a sardonic lilt underscoring its words. "Close enough, though. It still helped lead us back here."

"But, where exactly is 'here'?" he inquired, his voice tinged with apprehension.

"I'm certain you already know," came the reply, delivered in the same deadpan tone that sent shivers down his spine.

"Bergen Chrypt?"

"Is that the moniker you've bestowed upon this accursed place? I suppose it suffices. However, soon you shall acquaint yourself with its true essence."

As they traversed deeper into the heart of the valley, fragments of forgotten memories clawed their way to the forefront of his consciousness. Scenes of unspeakable horrors danced before his mind's eye, each more ghastly than the last. It was as if he was reliving a lifetime's worth of depraved acts with each heartbeat, a menagerie of unending nightmares from which there was no waking.

In the desolate expanse of the valley the sole structure remained shrouded in mystery, its presence ominous and foreboding. Closer inspection only heightened the sense of dread gnawing at his senses, as if the very air itself recoiled from the sight. Yet, despite his instincts screaming in protest, his feet continued to betray him, carrying him inexorably closer towards the enigmatic edifice. Desperation, again, clawed at his mind as he collapsed to his knees in a futile attempt to halt the relentless march toward an unknown fate. It was then that the Jackalope turned its gaze upon him with a voice like dry bones rattling in the wind.

"Come now, we're nearly there. You don't want to be late, do you?" its words dripped with a malevolent familiarity, each syllable a dissonant note in the symphony of terror that surrounded them. The thrum of its third eye bore down upon him, threatening to unravel the few fragile threads of his sanity that still remained.

Crawling on hands and knees, he pressed forward,

drawn toward the looming monolith that towered over him like a silent sentinel of ancient horrors. The word echoed in his mind, a whispered invocation of dread and despair–monolith. For a fleeting moment, he closed his eyes, steeling himself against the encroaching darkness. When he opened them again, the monolith stood before him, casting its oppressive shadow over his trembling form. As the Jackalope approached the base of the obsidian behemoth, its form seemed to waver and distort, swallowed by the abyssal depths of the structure's shadow. Like a ghost fading into the night the Jackalope vanished, leaving him to face the horrors of the monolith alone.

"You have come. After all of these years, you have finally come."

He felt the words reverberate within him, a primal ecstasy coursing through his veins, threatening to tear him asunder with its intensity. But defiance still flickered within his soul, a feeble flame against the encroaching darkness.

"Y-ye didn't give me much of a fuckin' choice, now, did ye?" His voice quivered, a mere whisper against the oppressive weight of the entity before him. He dared not meet its gaze, for fear of what horrors lurked within its depths.

"Did ye say . . . years?" he stammered, the realization sinking in like a dagger to his heart. "What tha fuck do ye want? What even are ye? What is this shit? Why me? For fuck's sake, why me?" The questions spilled from his lips like blood from a wound, his sanity teetering on the brink of oblivion. But the silence that followed was deafening, a void so absolute that it threatened to swallow him whole; and as he knelt there, his mind awash with uncertainty and dread, he dared to raise his gaze once more.

"Why me?" he pleaded, his voice a hollow echo in the void. But there was no answer, only the cold, unyielding winds of Bergen Chrypt. With trembling hands looked upon the towering obelisk, its surface etched with symbols of unspeakable horror. Each glyph danced before his eyes, twisting and contorting in an endless cycle of madness. He studied the eldritch edifice for what felt like a lifetime, and when he finally looked away the Monolith merely chuckled; a sound devoid of warmth or compassion.

"It has been so very long since I have had the pleasure of good company," it mused, its voice a sickening mockery of humanity. "I was simply hoping you would join me for a short chat."

"An' what exactly d' ye consider 'short'?" he snapped, the edges of his tone sharpened by a lifetime of doubt and disillusionment. "Ye say it's been years o' this shit, so let's get ta talkin' so's I can get home an' enjoy my supper." Yet, even as he spoke, a primal instinct within him whispered of the irreversible nature of the path he tread. His consciousness, a reluctant witness to the encroaching darkness, grappled with the realization of his own mortality. He felt the weight of his years bearing down upon him, a burden he could no longer deny, and as the obelisk beckoned with its insidious allure, the man found himself teetering on the precipice of revelation.

"Come now; we have so much to discuss. I wish to know more," the obelisk intoned, its voice a haunting melody that resonated within the depths of his being. Transfixed by the pulsating hues that danced along the surface of the ancient monument, the man struggled to find his voice amidst the chaos that engulfed him. His senses reeled, assaulted by the cacophony of unearthly sights and sounds that assailed him.

"Ah-ab-about whu-what?" he stammered, his words a feeble attempt to grasp hold of the rapidly unraveling reality before him. The very fabric of existence seemed to warp and bend, distorting his perception of time and space. Then, it came. A blinding eruption of light, tearing through the veil of darkness with an intensity that burned his very soul. The sky itself seemed to fracture, giving birth to a gaping maw of extra-spectral colors and psychedelic geometry awash in a sea of black stars. He could feel it calling to him, beckoning him into its embrace, its voracious hunger reaching out to claim him as its own. With a primal scream tearing through the air, the man was consumed by the swirling vortex of chaos. Reality warped and twisted around him, morphing into a nightmarish carnival of cosmic horror. Time lost all meaning as he was thrust into a maelstrom of incomprehensible terror. Scenes of unspeakable horror flashed before his eyes, each more grotesque than the last. Amidst the chaos, he saw himself– a spectral apparition, adrift in a sea of madness; his existence stretched thin, a mere puppet in the hands of forces beyond his understanding. The world around him fractured and splintered, twisting into impossible shapes that defied all reason. A wooden table, hastily constructed by unseen hands, morphed into an infernal altar of suffering; upon it lay a swine's head, its vacant eyes staring into eternity. But it was not merely flesh and bone that adorned the creature's visage. No, it was something far more sinister. Dripping with a vile ichor that reeked of rust and decay, mechanical limbs sprouted from the butchered head, turning it into something resembling an arachnid.

A primal scream echoed through the void as the abomination lunged forth, its mangled form a twisted parody of nature's design, and he shut his eyes in anticipation of the impending pain.

He blinked, but the world refused to focus. His eyelids fluttered like trapped moths against a light, struggling to keep pace with reality's rapid decay. When clarity returned, he knelt before the monolith, an obsidian pillar in a realm of shifting hues and alien geometry. The kaleidoscopic chaos around him resembled a hallucinogenic ocean, its waves crashing against the shores of his sanity. Tears welled in his eyes, not from fear, but from awe at the profound and cryptic beauty that enveloped him. This was no ordinary vision; it transcended the boundaries of perception, seeping into the marrow of his bones. Despite the surreal surroundings, a sense of eerie tranquility settled over him like a calm before the coming storm.

The entity before him spoke, its voice a discordant symphony of metallic echoes that reverberated through the air like broken thunder. "Oh, I see," it intoned, a hint of disappointment tainting its words. At its zenith an "eye" gleamed with an incandescent iridescence, its radiant gaze cascading like molten silver over the monolith's surface. As if in response to some arcane signal, the colossal structure began to contort and shrink, morphing into the likeness of a man. Transfixed, he watched the metamorphosis unfold, his curiosity eclipsing any semblance of fear. Approaching him with a lurching gait, the figure emerged from the fading shadows, a grotesque fusion of decay and vitality. Its form, encrusted with moss and adorned with withered bramble, exuded a sickly luminescence reminiscent of congealed blood. Beneath a tangled mane of oily hair, its eyes gleamed with an otherworldly intensity, their unnerving whiteness piercing through the darkness.

"What in the unholy fuck is this?" he wondered, the gravity of his predicament crashing down upon him like a tidal wave. The creature, once human yet now irrevocably transformed, advanced with an erratic rhythm that caused him to begin pleading, his momentary sense of safety now completely forgotten. Was it a demon? The thought lingered, but the truth felt far more elusive, veiled in the shadows of uncertainty. As it drew closer, the creature unleashed a deafening shriek, a cacophony of torment that tore through the fabric of reality itself. He recoiled with primal instinct, hands clamped over ears as though he were trying to crush his own skull. But it was pointless; a futile gesture against the inexorable tide of madness. In the throes of chaos he screamed, a primal cry torn from the depths of his soul; and in that moment of agonizing clarity, as his mind teetered once again on the brink of oblivion, he was wrenched from that damned place, torn from the grip of one nightmare only to be thrust into another, his sanity finally shattering like glass upon stone.

In the swirling mists of transformation he found himself reborn, not as a mere mortal, but as a primal force–a creature of ancient woods and forgotten rites. His essence intertwined with the very fabric of existence, a druid steeped in the mysteries of shape-shifting and arcane power. Through the verdant depths of the forest he roamed, drawn by an unseen force, seeking the secrets that lay hidden within the heart of the land. Before him stretched the yawning chasm, once vibrant with life but now twisted by some otherworldly influence. Its depths whispered of a power as old as time itself, beckoning him into its shaded embrace. With each step, he descended deeper into the dark valley, his mind consumed by visions of a reality beyond comprehension. Lost amidst the gnarled roots and tangled undergrowth, he stumbled into a realm untouched by mortal hands. Here, he would linger, ensnared by the siren song of an entity beyond human understanding. It spoke to him in colors and shapes, its voice echoing through the corridors of his mind like a concert of impossible images which defied mortal comprehension. Driven by a primal urge, he surrendered himself to the will of this cosmic parasite, his identity melding with its own until there was no distinction between them. Together, they would shape the land around them, bending reality to their whims with every flicker of thought. As the eons passed, they erected a monument made from a fallen meteor, a towering edifice that stood as a testament to their dominion over the land. But even as they basked in the glow of their creation, dark forces gathered on the horizon, drawn by the promise of untold power, for in the depths of the forest, where reality bled into madness, there were those who sought to challenge their reign: creatures of chaos and madness, driven by a hunger that could never be sated. So it was that the druid and his cosmic companion watched from their throne of stone as the world around them descended into chaos, and amidst the carnage they remained untouched; their bond unbreakable, their power unyielding–for they were the architects of this twisted reality, the guardians of its darkest secrets, and they would reign supreme until the end of time itself.

In the howling depths of Bergen Chrypt he found himself once more an outsider, a lone figure shrouded in the oppressive darkness. His eyes, haunted and hollow, fixated upon the towering monolith that loomed before him, its ethereal silhouette casting a pall over the desolate landscape. The demonlike entity, a warped amalgamation of madness, shifted and writhed before him, its forms morphing between that of the Jackalope, the blood-faced man, and other eldritch horrors beyond mortal comprehension. Its gaze bore into his soul with a disapproving intensity.

"Tsk, tsk," it chided, its voice now dripping a chilling mockery of sympathy. "I had hoped for better from you, my friend. I have looked into the deepest recesses of your soul, and I have determined that while I do like bees, I do not think I like you." The last words held a sharpness that gave an intense weight to the silence which followed. Caught off guard, his mind raced with a torrent of conflicting emotions. Without hesitation, he blurted out in a desperate attempt to break the suffocating silence.

"What about that rat-faced fuck? Why not him? Why didn't you bring him here to be yer friend?" The entity seemed to regard him with an odd indifference.

"He served his purpose, as you will serve yours. The

cycle of fate is unyielding, and none can escape its grasp." His heart pounded with a primal fear as he struggled to comprehend the entity's cryptic words.

"Please," he pleaded, his voice trembling with uncertainty. "Let me go back to my life, to my wife. I ain't no good at conversation, an' I'm a lousy friend." But his pleas fell on deaf ears, for the entity's gaze bore into him with an intensity that chilled him to the bone. "You have deceived me," it declared, its voice devoid of emotion. "And for that, you shall suffer."

In an instant, reality itself seemed to unravel before his eyes, replaced by a kaleidoscopic tapestry of nightmares that tore at the fabric of his sanity. He was plunged into an alien realm where the laws of reality held no sway, where every shadow whispered of unspeakable horrors. As he drifted through this churning landscape, he was confronted with a grim reflection of his own past–a scene of violence and despair that unfolded before his eyes with a cruel clarity. He watched helplessly as his past self, consumed by rage and despair, inflicted unspeakable horrors upon his own wife, leaving her scarred physically for weeks, and emotionally for a lifetime. He was forced to relive every second of it from this naked perspective.

He felt filthy. He felt sick. He felt wrong.

In that moment of agonizing clarity, he realized the true nature of his torment: he was not merely a pawn in a game of fate, but a prisoner of his own mind, condemned to wander the twisted labyrinth of his own nightmares for all eternity.

He found himself next within a dimly lit tavern in Schleswig, amidst the stench of sweat and spilled ale, ensnared in a high-stakes match of Dead Man's Double–a game where fortunes were wagered and souls were lost. He had gambled recklessly, and the dice had betrayed him, leaving him in bitter defeat. In a fit of rage he plunged his blade into the heart of the victor, the metallic tang of blood mingling with the acrid scent of fear. His actions were fueled by a primal urge, an insatiable hunger for retribution, and as the life drained from his victim he reveled in twisted satisfaction–yipping and hollering in a drug-fueled stupor which urged him to piss on the dead man's cards before collecting his ill-gotten gains.

His descent into darkness did not end there. Next, he watched himself behind a brothel, amidst the filth and decay, choking the life out of a hapless prostitute, her pleas for mercy drowned out by the cacophony of the surrounding debauchery. In another memory now, under the cold light of day, he hurled venomous words at his wife and berated her for overcoming the beans before raising the back of his hand to her in a threatening gesture. The passage of time became meaningless, a blur of anguish and despair. Memories, like specters from the past, haunted his every waking moment, tormenting him with their cruel clarity. Each recollection was a dagger to his soul, a reminder of the darkness that lurked within.

Bile crept up from the depths of his gut, a foul tide threatening to drown him from within. Doubled over, retching, the world around him twisted and warped, reality itself slipping through his fingers like sand in an hourglass. When the convulsions ceased, he found himself back in his own pasture, hand in hand with his wife, dancing through memories like ghosts through a mist. They tended to their garden, the bees buzzing around them like loyal subjects, each named and cherished. He watched as he patted his mule's flank, felt the roughness of its fur beneath his touch, heard the soft crunch of the apple as it crumbled in his hand. Silver exchanged between old comrades, a bond forged in the crucible of war. He relieved hundreds of pleasant memories, then a thousand more, as a happiness taken for granted played out before for a lifetime; and under the weight of this new revelation the idyllic facade shattered, giving way to a nightmare. Memories shifted and cascaded like a torrent pulling him inward, each one more twisted than the last, until he found himself once again kneeling before the monolith. The ever-changing landscape taunted him, mocking his feeble attempts to grasp reality. How could anyone hope to navigate this labyrinth of madness?

"Now you see," the entity intoned, a shadow in the void, "Was it worth it?"

"N-n-no," his voice faltered, defiance warring with terror. "No, damnit! NO! WHAT IS THIS? WHAT THE FUCK IS THIS?" His jaw clenched, muscles straining against the tide of insanity threatening to engulf him. Tears of blood trickled down his cheeks, his eyes bulging with the strain.

"Shhh," it whispered, a mockery of comfort. "Shhhhh, shhhhhh, shhhhhh shhhhhhhhhh . . . " But beneath the facade of reassurance lay a deeper menace, and within his mind a primal terror emerged that allowed him to cling to the last vestiges of his sanity.

"Fuck y-ye, whatever ye are!" he spat, defiance mingled with despair. "I DON'T BELONG HERE! YE DON'T BELONG HERE! GET OUT OF MY HEAD!" The entity's laughter echoed through the void, a cacophony of insane sounds that threatened to consume him whole.

"I'm your new best friend," it crooned, a serpent's hiss wrapped in honeyed words, "whether you like it or not. Honestly, whether I like it or not. You're here for a while. Quite a while, unfortunately. Perhaps you would like to join me inside of my head?" But he would not submit, not without a fight. With a guttural scream, he defied the darkness, clinging to the frayed edges of reality as the void threatened to consume him whole. "LET ME GO," he yelled. It wasn't a plea, but a command. His stomach quivered and his bowels shuddered, and he felt his blood go thin as if he was about to pass out.

In the haze of consciousness that lingered he couldn't discern whether he had passed out or if reality had simply melted away. Lowering his elbow revealed a barren landscape, devoid of all but the desolation that echoed through the marrow of this hollow land. No towering monoliths, no crimson cloaked figures, no eldritch horrors danced on the edges of perception; only the oppressive weight of Bergen Chrypt itself. Rising to his feet, he spun in frustrated circles, searching for a beacon of hope amidst the oppressive gloom, only to find a weathered pedestal–its obsidian surface coated in a layer of dust and decay. The searing pain pierced his skull anew, and as his trembling fingers explored the wound, feeling the jagged shard wet with fresh blood. Panic welling inside of him again, he pulled hard at the piece of stone until was dislodged with a slick unsheathing sound. A fresh gout of dark blood melted down his face like hot wax, followed by an intense throbbing that caused the vision in his left eye to streak with tendrils of blurred light. Driven only by the instinct to escape, he fled into the surrounding darkness, heedless of the jagged terrain that tore at his flesh with each agonizing step. Every stumble, every fall, only fueled his desperation as he sought refuge from the horrors that besieged him. At last, he crested a ridge, leaving the valley of nightmares behind him, and there he stumbled upon a cavern–a sanctuary amidst the madness.

With trembling hands, he kindled a meager fire, its flickering light offering some semblance of comfort in this wretched hellscape. Yet, as he gazed into its depths, he beheld a vision that caused his stomach to drop: within the heart of the flames danced a spectral apparition, its gaze burning with an otherworldly intensity. Terror gripped him as he recoiled from the unearthly spectacle, his voice trembling with disbelief and dread. "What the fuck is this now? Have I not suffered enough?" he cried, his words echoing through the small cavern. The voice that answered him was as cold and unyielding as the grave, its words carrying the weight of untold eons.

"You thought to escape your sins, but they have followed you here, as they always do. There is no escape from the darkness that dwells within you." With a deafening roar, the flames surged forth, engulfing him in a world of flame. As the world dissolved into a maelstrom of fire and shadow, he realized with a sinking heart that his torment had only just begun.

When his vision cleared he found himself planted firmly back in his own front yard, a witness to the mundane activities of rural life: goats grazed lazily, the mule ambled about in its pen, and bees darted to and fro around their hives. Yet, an unsettling fog lingered in his mind, obscuring the events that led him to this peculiar moment.

"What just happened?" he muttered to himself, his voice barely a whisper against the backdrop of the eerie calm. His gaze darted around the familiar surroundings, searching for clues, when he noticed a rabbit staring at him from the brush. Then, like a dissonant chord in an otherwise harmonious melody, his wife's voice pierced the silence.

"D'yeh think yeh'd like ta try some fruited boar fat with cream fer dessert?" Her words dripped with an unsettling sweetness, a veneer of normalcy masking something sinister beneath. "I heard from Salizu that it's real good, and I think you'd like it." Her presence caused him to shiver, her figure a twisted distortion of familiarity as she went about her chores. But it was her words that chilled him to the core, laden with a threat that hung heavy in the air.

"Besides," she continued, her tone taking on a mocking edge, "if you don't eat it, I'll just remove your face with your favorite hunting knife, you stupid ass-loving buffoon!" A macabre laughter bubbled forth from her lips, the sound scraping against his sanity like nails on a chalkboard. As she turned to face him, her features contorted into the grotesque caricature he had run away from, painted in hues of blood and malice. As he fell to his knees he noticed the figure lurking at the edge of the forest, a doppelgänger of himself staring back with eyes wide with terror. The realization dawned upon him like a creeping shadow: they were not alone.

The thing wearing his wife's skin drew closer, its visage lacking lips, its voice a hollow echo of the woman he once knew.

"Like I told you," it intoned, each word dripping with a chilling finality, "a long time. A very, very long time."

Within the desolate depths of the Bergen Chrypt, deep in a forgotten canyon where even monsters dare not travel, he lay sprawled upon the unforgiving terrain, a decrepit figure forsaken by time and memory. His weathered frame contorted in grotesque spasms, his vacant eyes rolled dangerously far back into his head as foam poured from the corners of his mouth. His limbs jerked at odd angles. At times, he went stiff, then would begin to move and twitch again. He mumbled and moaned about nothing that made sense.

Blending seamlessly with the shadows cast by the towering monolith, a three-eyed Jackalope looked on in amusement.

I, MYCELIUM

HARLEN LINKE

THE BOG WIZARD arose much as he did every other day: naked, disoriented in a haze of eminent sobriety, and head pounding to the rhythm of the previous night's drum ritual.

He leaned over the edge of his rugged driftwood-framed bed and vomited, tasting the fermented saprotrophic tea brewed the week before to dull any awareness of reality. The awareness that was crushing in like a falling tree.

How I despise this, was his first coherent thought of the day.

He reached a withered hand out for the small side table, but missed and tumbled from the moss-covered bed, onto the damp wooden floor. In the moment before the pain rushed in to greet him, he noted the similarity in sound to a wet leather bag of sticks getting dropped in front of a hearth.

His skeletal gray hand shot up onto the table and prodded around until finding purchase on a long wooden pipe and dragged it back where he lay in a crumpled heap. The orange glow of a small flame appeared on his opposing fingertip, igniting the dregs of the pipe. The Bog Wizard inhaled deep, held for a moment, and exhaled a plume of acrid purple smoke, filling the room with the familiar haze.

Rolling onto his back with a creak, he examined the contents of the pipe, dumping ashes across his long flowing white beard in the process. With a bedraggled lip-smack, the venerable man sat up, now seeming to possess the strength to at least get that far. After a moment of thought, he began to again scour the table, knocking over various bottles and trinkets. A small well-worn brown leather pouch was found and snatched up. Sliding two fingers into the pouch and feeling around, he frowned. A ridiculously small pinch of dried purple leaf was removed from the bag and delicately placed into the pipe, before being once again ignited and inhaled.

With a plop, a fat green and red toad hopped into the open front door of the shack and croaked, breaking the silence.

"I *know* I should've planned ahead!" the Bog Wizard growled at the amphibian, who leaped back in a panic. The effort of speech pushed him into a coughing fit until he hacked a large ball of phlegm onto the floor.

How much of the plant did I use last night? I had enough to last the next week, he thought.

A threadbare dark purple robe was gruffly yanked off the end of the bed. He pushed his thin bony arms through the sleeves. His light gray skin was riddled with pockmarks and scars, catching the morning light through the small round window of his hut, his gaunt frame highlighted by ribs protruding under thin leathery flesh. He braced himself on the bed frame and got up with a groan, pulling the thick robe closed and tying it with a large leather belt. Shuffling across the room and bending down, he picked up his gnarled wooden staff. The vague recollection of throwing it unceremoniously across the room the night before as he fell into the bed flashed across his mind.

Now leaning his full weight on the staff, his back was hunched enough that his beard scraped across his knees. His long gray hair was half tucked into the robe and half messily draped across his back. It was riddled with sticks and leaves, and a small patch of brown mushrooms appeared to be growing out of the top of his scalp where his hair was thinner. His bulbous gray nose was veined blue and purple; his eyes were solid milky white with a blue glow emanating from the edges.

A faint pulsing hum originated from the naturally formed wooden staff. It was long, with a large knot on the end, not only walking aid, but a channel for his power, and a cudgel as needed. While he stood hunched and supported by it, the staff rose slightly taller than the wizard himself.

He shambled his way towards a large iron pot with faint embers glowing under it, hanging from a wooden frame. He threw on a log from the pile, with little thought to where it landed. It was instantly engulfed with a flash of blue flame, settling to a steady orange roar. The pot began bubbling shortly after. Inside was a thick, greenish-brown goo, with various unidentifiable meats and detritus dotting it. The wizard scooped up a handful of speckled mushrooms from a wicker basket and tossed them in. He shakily hovered over the pot, occasionally stirring the slimy stew. With a creaky popping stretch and a yawn, he ladled a portion of the conglomeration into a clay bowl, and sat at a rickety table.

After sloppily devouring the bowlful, he went to a bookshelf of leather-bound tomes and began poring over them, puffing on a different wooden pipe, strategically placed in anticipation of his morning routine. With another frown, he exhaled the plain gray smoke out of his nose and pondered it.

Disappointing, he thought.

It reminded him of the Time Before, as he had come to call it. The time before he was the Bog Wizard, when he had been something else.

Over the years, it had come together in pieces, but it was all a hazy and vague memory of long ago. He had determined his origins were druidic in nature, with a strong connection to the swamp. The swamp had always been there, the one constant.

What he was sure of, though, was that something bad happened. Some ancient power turned on that person from Before, pulling him into the swamp, destroying him and dominating his mind.

That was the moment things went blank. A slice of death, nothingness. He became a slave to the power, the power that was drawing on the swamp, doing its bidding. Untold time passed during this state, hundreds of years at least. His body, which should have long perished, continued.

Eventually, a sliver of consciousness re-emerged. At first, he was trapped within his mind, but he felt encouraged to push harder by some other force, some third and external force, seemingly of the swamp itself. Exerting his will, he began to regain control, fighting the ancient power into submission, leveraging the very swamp against it. Combining them, and rising as The Bog Wizard.

In a cosmic twist of insufferable irony, after gaining his freedom from the ancient power that once controlled him, he then found himself tethered to the swamp. Drawing his strength from it. Existing in an undead state far past his time. Leaving its confines and entering dry land would quickly sap him; with extensive testing, he determined he would succumb within an hour or so outside of the embrace of the mire.

Re-death, how boring, the thought, closing the book abruptly, sending dust motes and spores spiraling into the thick smoke. *The past is just that.*

A sensation like that of a twig snapping inside of his mind made him aware of an intrusion into the swamp. Scooping up his staff, he charged out with an unnatural speed for his frail form.

Over the years, he had formed a bond with the swamp and the mycorrhizal network it contained. He drew power from it but also became part of it, in ways. Its tendrils ran deep into the wet soil, an interlacing of roots and fungus connecting it all. What the swamp knew, he knew. If the swamp fell, so would he.

He trudged through murky waters, submerged waist deep while leaving a silent wake behind him. The swamp moved around him, helping push him along, all manner of flora and fauna parting in front of him. The animals fell silent, even the insects ceasing their chirps and buzzes, all taking a moment to watch their protector on the move.

A tidal wave of sludge formed behind him, raising him as he approached the interlopers, a grubby pair tending to a broken cart. At a glance, it seemed as if their horse had startled and run into the bog, only to lodge the cart's wheels deep in the muck before bursting free. A disturbed channel in the scum showed the horse's path of escape.

Smart animal, he thought, a devilish grin flashing over his face.

"Get out of my BOG!"

The words thundered, seemingly from every direction, with the roar of a thousand angry voices.

The spell was simple, but flashy. It served as a great way to disorient and panic a target, instilling a sense of dread, and would often be enough on its own to scare off intruders altogether, adding to the lore of the swamp and keeping the local villagers away.

One of the carters—tall but skinny, wearing basic leather scraps, with dark shaggy hair and a graying beard, a well-worn sword sheath on his hip—jumped nearly out of his skin. "RUN!" he shouted to the other, much shorter, and bare-faced.

He could have just let them go, but today, he decided to take a more direct approach, to remind them of the power here.

At his command, a great wave surged, washing over the stuck cart, crushing it further into the mire. Both carters were swept violently off their feet. The smaller one's head collided with a tree, crunching, spraying its contents, becoming part of the muck.

Shorter, smaller, bare-faced . . . young? Is that the term? the Bog Wizard pondered.

The other man was hardier. Righting himself, wiping his eyes of slime, he drew his sword. Its blade was dented and damaged. Garbage. Scavengers.

"We will not die like this, demon!" the man shouted in a defiant, almost priestly manner. His eyes darted around, looking for the other, a look of despair wrenching his mud-splattered face.

The Bog Wizard perched atop of the remains of the cart, grinning maniacally, and let out a deep guttural growl. *"Wrong."*

He gestured casually with his staff. A pulsing blue energy formed at the bulbous tip and three blue-white wisps shot towards the man. The first struck the arm holding his sword, exploding, dropping both hand and weapon into the swamp. The second hit him in the opposing knee, splaying his leg apart and knocking him down. The last sank directly into his chest. The man appeared to briefly bulge from within, then blood spouted from his mouth and nose. He collapsed, sinking slowly.

The wizard inhaled deeply, and the bog exhaled with him, the source of tension now subdued. All was again peaceful, the birds and insects singing their praises. A large, toothy crocodile who had been spectating the events smiled in approval, turned with a splash, and slinked away.

This had always been his task, to prevent others from trespassing, by any means necessary. Whenever man or savage beast made a push, he was right there to push back, not allowing them to take any ground.

As civilization grew and encroached, he had to devise new ways to defend his realm, conjuring giant golems to do his bidding. These hulking creatures were amalgamations of mud, mulch, bone, and waterlogged wood, the very essence of the swamp. They were dumb and only knew of violence, but he could at least point them in a direction and set them loose to cause havoc until their power waned, bringing the wrath of the swamp down upon the villages whenever they dared to step too far. It always sent a great message.

Placing a gentle withered hand on a nearby tree, he closed his eyes, penetrating mentally deeper into the immeasurable matrices of mycelium mosaics underfoot, to the vast swamp and the creatures that belonged to it. Twisting his neck to one side with a loud crack, he inhaled the miasma of putrid mire.

His mind itched with sobriety, and it felt like suffering.

The purple plant, he thought exasperatedly. The need left a gaping hole in him, not a problem that would solve itself. Ironically, the plant thrived in a drier environment than the heart of the bog provided, and all his efforts to cultivate it had failed. It longed to be in the wild, which he respected. Luckily, it grew towards the northern edges of his territory, where it could be obtained with minimal risk, and regrow before it was needed again.

Although, he thought, *this may be a bit early to harvest another batch . . .*

Opting for a less dramatic travel method, the wizard climbed out of the knee-high muck onto firmer land, and began his trek to the north, shambling along steadily, gnarled staff in hand. By mid-day, a cool breeze swept through the stagnant air, stirring up insects. Some would find him interesting and land on his exposed skin, perhaps attempting to bite. After failing to pierce his leathery old hide, not that they would find much of value under it, they would simply fly away.

His thoughts were on the plant. The sweet, delicious purple leaf. When inhaled, it filled his reality with visions, seeming even to enhance his magical capabilities. Without it, however, he felt lost. His mind writhed in agony longing for it. But the feeling seemed to be mutual; it appeared the soggy old wizard was the only one the plant cared for as well. He had witnessed weaker minds attempt to partake in it, only to be turned into drooling messes, their mental faculties permanently corroded.

Their loss, he justified, smiling grimly.

A few hours into the trek, his footing became firmer as

the uliginous earth receded behind him. With every step further he could feel the swamp a little less than the previous. It was a dry, uneasy feeling, like leaving oneself behind. The hardness of the ground was an uncomfortable, unstable feeling. Nothing held on to you as you walked, you were on your own, riding along the top, balancing on the edge.

Dotted here and there were small budlings of vibrant purple leaves, but the telltale signs of a ripe harvest were lacking. These were immature and not ready to be plucked. They needed more time, time that he did not have. He would have to move further out and hope to find older plants. The quality would be poor, but it would work for the time being.

A crack in the soil caught his eye. He stopped mid-stride and crouched to investigate. It had not rained in about a week and the land was dry. He dug a few knotted fingers into the crack until he found moisture, forming a small pool around his jagged, mud-caked fingernails. He closed his eyes and concentrated on the trillions of roots and mycelium below. The dense system, branching off and communicating to everything around him. The trees passing nutrients between them to help each other survive, warning of dangers, taking care of each other.

Ahead of him lay nothingness, and behind him was everything.

Standing up, he allowed the moisture to drip off his fingers before taking another step. He could feel the weight of his body beginning to press down on him harder. His long-atrophied muscles strained to continue.

This is the line, he thought, *where the bog ends.*

Checking the sun's position relative to the trees, he began a timer in his head. He inhaled deep and held his breath briefly, then resumed walking. Leaning harder on his cane with every step, he became more hunched, more drained.

He continued to see the young, immature plants

sparsely dotting the landscape. His vision began to blur as he strained to keep them focused.

Ahead was a hill, the hill that had, on previous trips, been the marker between wet and dry, between power and weakness.

Just getting to the top should provide, he thought, grimacing. *I just have to make it a little further and I can turn back. I need this.*

"I need this," he repeated aloud in a scratchy whisper.

Approaching the apex of the hill, he let out a groan of despair. The plants were nowhere in sight. He collapsed onto his hands and knees, looking closely at the ground, fingering at a loose indentation in the soil, which had been disrupted and then stomped. Someone had pulled the plant, roots and stem, and hastily tried covering it up. A set of tracks led away, pawprints with five sharp claws.

Perhaps there had been other intruders? Men he had not sensed, who had an animal of some kind with them" He searched for more information, but his mind was beginning to struggle.

Then he glimpsed a familiar vibrant purple color, down the other side of the hill, spotting among the green and brown blur the forest had begun to take on as his vision worsened further. He began crawling that way, backwards on all fours, staff in hand. He wasn't sure if it was possible for him to stand at this point, and he didn't want to risk a fall, or expend too much energy before the return trip.

Just one good plant, that will get me through, he thought, his beard catching on the tall grass.

A scratching, scrabbling noise from behind gave him pause. As he attempted to rise and turn, his ailing body failed him and he lost his balance, tumbling backwards down the hill. His collar bone snapped with a loud, reverberant pop. He landed chest first onto a pile of loose gravel, the less than graceful thud knocking the wind from him. Gasping for air, he painfully rolled to his side . . . and came face to face with his goal.

The beautiful purple plant, in all its mature glory! Its acrid scent teased him between desperate gasps for breath. He stretched an aching arm over a leathery, snake-like vine, but was suddenly jerked flat onto his back.

Two pointed, whiskered faces looked down on him with disgust, red eyes flanking long snouts punctuated by big, pointed teeth. Ragged ears poked from under leather hoods. One of them wielded a club made of bone, apparently the femur of some humanoid.

These Ratlings are taking my flowers! he thought in a panic, before the club struck a heavy blow to his head and he blacked out.

My flowers! he thought again, as he returned from the haze of unconsciousness.

His head throbbed, pounding him into an awakened state. Attempting to open his eyes, he realized they already were, but he still could not see. His arms were pinned, both legs also locked into place. Rolling his head on his neck, his jaw pulled open, and he let out a weak cough.

The hood of his robe fell back and unobscured his eyes. A blaze of orange dancing light blurred his vision as he groggily took in his surroundings. He was bound to a wooden chair with hempen rope, his robe bunched up between the mess of hastily tied knots. His ankles were tied tightly to the legs of the chair, his hands bound behind him. The pain in his contorted shoulder reminded him of the fall he suffered, and how close he had come to his precious purple flowers before—-

"Ratlings!" he spat.

He was in a ramshackle hut made of straw and wood. The contents of his pockets had been laid out on a table: A small pouch of spell reagents, his traveling pipe, a handful of red acorns, and a blue obsidian stone. His pocket-sized alligator leather spell book scribed with ancient sigils down the scaly spine had been tossed to the floor, beside a charred dark stain of blood, and the blown-out soles of two leather boots.

He smirked faintly. *At least something still had a little power left in it,* he thought.

The ancient grimoire's warding spell would destroy anyone who opened its cover improperly, and it had clearly taken out at least one of the creatures that had been scavenging his gear. It, unfortunately, was a one-time enchantment, but seemed to have at least scared off his captors and bought him some time.

Time! he suddenly remembered.

He had lost track of how long he had been out of his swamp, but judging from the dim light entering the hut, it had definitely been far too long. He shifted his bones as much as he could in the bonds. The gritty crunch of his joints indicated he was drying out, losing what little power remained by the minute, the eternal void beckoning.

Interrupting the Bog Wizard's bodily check, a short, slender figure appeared in the doorway and sneered a sharp, toothy muzzle at him. It uttered a few words in a scratchy sharp language he didn't understand, but sounded full of contempt. The creature was touching the unmistakable hilt of a blade originally belonging to someone of status, its ornate polished pommel sticking up in an awkward way from an ill-fitting belt. These beasts were clearly scavengers and ambushers, having taken anything of use or value from locals weak and pathetic enough to fall into their traps.

Another rat-like figure appeared behind the first, this one much more rotund, holding a wicker basket and greedily devouring the contents. The wizard sniffed the air, detecting a faint, familiar aroma. Through his fading vision, he saw dark red stains on the mouth of the fat rat as it sloppily gnashed away.

"Blood berries . . . from *my* bog . . . " he uttered hoarsely.

The two figures looked at each other, their ears angling forward to take in more sound.

"*MY* bog . . . *MY* berries!" he said, summoning what little energy he contained to project his voice before going into another coughing fit, much to the delight of the rat creatures, who began to cackle shrill, squeaky laughs in his direction.

Then the larger one stopped laughing and lunged, punching him in the gut with its free hand, basket clutched tight with the other. A few berries bounced out during the vicious attack, and rolled off somewhere below the chair. The fat rat laughed again as the wizard sputtered for breath, its companion again joining in the shrill cackle.

The wizard spotted a bulbous red orb just to the side of his foot. Inside that beautiful berry was power . . . not much, but just enough he could possibly utilize it to turn the odds. With his ankle bound tightly to the chair, it didn't allow for the movement necessary to reach the berry. Even splaying his smallest toe as far as he could, he was still nowhere near the red sphere.

He relaxed, closed his eyes, and inhaled deep.

Roaring, he flexed every decaying muscle he could focus on. Biting down on his tongue, he tasted the thick black substance that passed for his blood. His ankle cracked once, then again, a sharp bone fragment protruding from the skin. He rotated his foot closer to the berry, still screaming and thrashing to distract the Ratlings. They gaped at him, bewildered, not noticing until too late his painfully contorted foot bringing the ragged nail of his smallest toe into contact with the berry.

Power!

A blinding flash filled the hut, an explosion of force erupting. The larger, closer Ratling's legs were swept out from under it, flesh from the lower half of its body ripping away and pelting the smaller one lurking further back. The chair legs splintered, along with nearly every bone below the wizard's knees. The blast hurled him backwards, the seat splitting beneath his scrawny rump. He landed hard, fragmenting the chair's back, cracking his spine, and loosening his restraints.

The wizard summoned what little energy he had left to shake off the tangled ropes, dragging himself semi-sitting to survey the damage. The fat Ratling's entrails were heaped in a pool of blood. The smaller, matted with gory debris, stood frozen in shock.

Crawling on his forearms, legs dragging behind him, the wizard plunged his hands into steaming Ratling guts and started feeling around for any remnants of the basket of berries, which had vanished during the explosion. The Ratling in the doorway spun away and vomited with a squelch, then fled, horrified and staggering.

Elbow-deep in slippery viscera, arms stiffening as damage and decay warred with his will, head and eyelids going heavy, he slumped face-first toward the mess, about to succumb to what he knew would be the final darkness.

A pokey mesh of sodden twigs against his fingertips told him he was touching part of the sought-after basket. He scrabbled through organs and found a single firm globule.

Pinching it with desperate, weak fingers, he rolled out of the stinking innards, pulling his arms free. With his last ounce of strength, utilizing the momentum of the roll, he brought his hand up and, through the tangled bloody mess of hair and beard overwhelming his face, stuffed the berry into his mouth.

He closed his eyes, on the verge of losing consciousness, and bit. Sweet juice squirted down his throat, and he snapped his eyes open again. With newfound energy, the Bog Wizard snatched up his spell book and other belongings—of his staff, there was no sign—and crawled for the door, his lower legs still in ruins.

The berry would only sustain him for a brief amount of time. Casting a spell in this condition would likely be his end. He needed to get back to his swamp.

Where am I? How far did they take me? How long have I got? he wondered frantically as he scrabbled from the hut, his useless legs dragging behind him in streaks of blood.

A fresher breeze hit his face and chilled him. He was outside, free, but the sun was far too low.

A pot bubbled over a small makeshift fire pit. surrounded by empty stools. A few cups, some overturned with contents spilled, suggested the others had cleared out in a hurry.

I practically fell into their camp, he marveled, recognizing nearby the same hill he'd first climbed and then tumbled down.

A Ratling emerged from another hut, wielding a bone club. It hissed, stalking menacingly toward him.

His mind flashed back to his initial encounter with that club, one he was not eager to repeat. He saw his staff, leaning against a log on the other side of the fire pit, but shook his head, knowing it was too far and he was too weak to properly wield it anyway. Crawling closer to the fire pit, he recognized the potent scent of strong alcohol, and fumbled for one of the still-upright cups, praying it was full.

The Ratling charged, club raised, ready to deal a blow that would surely be the end.

There were no second chances here. Filling his mouth with the bitter, potent liquid, he plunged his other hand into the firepit. As the Ratling loomed over him, club beginning its swing, he yanked his charred hand from the fire, holding a fistful of glowing embers. He opened his palm and spat a spray of alcohol across it. The spray ignited into a gout of flame, squarely in the Ratling's face. It fell back, screaming, dropping its club. It rolled around, flailing, trying to put out its burning fur in the surrounding dirt. The wizard casually tossed the remaining contents of the cup onto it, fanning the flames into an explosive roar.

The Ratling's screams grew shriller and more desperate, but the wizard ignored them, focusing on his goal: his staff on the far side of the fire pit. He crawled over and took hold of it, using it for leverage to work his way closer to the hill, his only shot at salvation.

The hill, and the purple plants dotting its slope.

I'll grab some on the way by, get over the hill, and be in the clear. Then regroup, maybe send a golem to get revenge on anyone left in this dismal hole, he told himself, encouragingly.

His strength faltered, every inch forward seeming harder than the previous. The berry's potency was wearing off. But the faint scent of the purple plant drove him on, as the Ratling's shrieks faded to a deafening silence.

Reaching the first plant in his path, he grasped at it. Even the sticky thorns digging into his hand was a comfort. He pulled weakly, bending the thick stalk, the thorns piercing deeper, the purple flowers tantalizingly close. He tugged harder, feeling his grip weaken.

Just one, he thought. *Just give me one for now—*

Someone flipped him onto his back and he came face to face with the smaller Ratling, the one who'd vomited in the doorway. It held the ornate hilted sword he'd noticed earlier, a sneer on its face. Before he could react, it jabbed the point into his chest, eliciting a faint, stunted gasp. Snarling fiercely, the Ratling leaned and twisted, plunging the blade clear through to the dry grass and earth underneath.

When the Ratling pulled it free, thick black blood oozed from the wound. The Ratling let out a screechy, triumphant roar, turning back towards the camp and away from its conquered foe.

The wizard clutched at his chest, attempting to scoop the leaking sludge back in.

Not like this; not yet, not so close, he thought, with a yearning look at the miasmic purple plant, rustling, mocking his failure. His eyes rolled back in his head as he released his hold on the mortal plane.

The thick black liquid sank into the ground beneath him, soaking into the soil. Deep in the damper underground, the roots began to take notice, squirming. Tiny tendrils of mycelium stretched towards the moisture, towards its family, its own. The entire network desperately attempted to reconnect to its protector. The bog needed him, just as he needed the bog. It knew this, it always knew this, and, therefore, the wizard always knew this.

The underground web of fungus sought out the decaying liquid death, drinking it in. It hungrily searched for more, a mesh forming behind it, pushing it up further through the soil. It extruded into the flesh of the rotting man, filling the gaps the sword had made and feeding on the necrotic flesh within.

The wizard suddenly and violently arched his back, his body a taut bow balanced on his broken legs and head. He gasped for air. His skull throbbed and burned as new nerves and synapses formed within, the mycelium strands reconnecting pathways in his brain. He seized, limbs thrashing.

The Ratling whirled, raising its sword, only to recoil, alarmed, as the wizard floated into the air, a hazy green glow surrounding him. A bright white light burst from his eyes and mouth. His arms flew wide, his staff circling around him in a wide loop, pulsing with blue energy.

The wizard tilted his head, meeting the gaze of the now terrified Ratling, who dropped its plundered sword and turned to run. A humming blue energy gloved the wizard's hands, coalesced into a crackling ball in front of him, and shot at the fleeing creature. The Ratling exploded into a cloud of blood and fur, bone shrapnel peppering the terrain with a thousand tiny puffs of dust.

Then, the wizard revolved in the air, gesturing with his staff. A dozen purple plants pulled their roots free from the soil, following him as he floated up over the hill.

Reaching the edge of the swamp's moister ground, he descended, his dangling feet dragging in the mire, returning to a more controlled, fully conscious state. He dropped into a murky pool, sinking in up to his nose, eyes closing in bliss as his body shivered and absorbed strength from the liquid. As he basked there, meditating, the plants circled his hovering staff, patient and obedient.

I, MYCELIUM

Things were different now; that much he knew. He had changed somehow, changed in ways he needed to assess, to determine what his new limits were, and what, if any, abilities he might have gained. He no longer felt the *need* for the purple plant, but he understood that he still *wanted* it. It was a subtle distinction, but one that gave him comfort. He had made some mistakes in his quest for it before; its draw was too great.

He felt a somehow even stronger connection to the swamp, sensing the fungus within him, making him more a part of it than ever. He even found himself able to remember more of his own past; the swamp had been there to see it, so he could now see it.

Yes, there he had been, back in that time, a living man, his flesh whole and warm and tanned, venturing into the swamp, harvesting its bounty of fruits and plants. His shovel had pierced the damp soil, digging a bit too greedily for a power he had yet to understand.

Another mistake he had made.

Opening his eyes, he smiled, welcoming the night. He emerged from the bog, washed of the blood and guts, with fresh green algae coating his hair and beard. His legs, although wobbly and still not entirely solid, seemed stable enough to walk on, with aid. His gnarled wooden staff floated to his side and settled into his hand.

He beckoned the plants, and they followed as he began walking towards home.

His first order of business would be to begin the drying process of the purple flowers. Needed or not, craved or not, he could still enjoy and benefit from its effects.

The second order of business involved whipping up a few golems, sending one to the Ratling camp to clean up any stragglers, and others to all the nearby villages.

They had all clearly gotten too comfortable pushing close to his swamps, and they needed to be punished.

So the Bog Wizard saw; so the Bog Wizard knew.

SCREAMS OF THE NECROPOLIS

JOHN BALTISBERGER

I

THE LITTLE TAVERN in Postek was dirty. They were always dirty; it was a sign of the times, or rather, of the way people reacted to the times. Why bother sweeping when tomorrow might bring the misery that brings upheaval destroying all you have ever known? It was nonsensical, not that life made any sense anyway. Upheaval and tragedy were nothing new to the world; the Two that were two, those damned Basilisks, did not invent pain and catastrophe. They merely sang its song the loudest.

Of course, they had help. The choir of idiots of Josilfa's Church lined up to worship the heralds of the last days. You may not be able to stop the end of all things, and you may not be able to predict it, but you could at least let a man get drunk in peace.

Dödz sat at the bar, staring into the distinct lack of foam in his beer. Flatter than the blade of a well-kept axe. But it still had some kick, and at the moment, that was all he cared about. He had left Kergis behind, along with the rest of those he had served with. Just more frozen corpses to warn others about testing their luck against the elements and monstrosities of that place.

He had seen companions and comrades die before—and die as badly, if not worse than they had as he hunted Lady Crol—but what bothered him was the prophecies he had heard in his dreams, whispered by a lich intent on bringing the dying world under his hand.

"We are given the world in icy death and burning damnation. The mistress and the master joined in the hollow place. They lead the way to a darkness unseen by all but the blind. And in that place they open a thousand mouths to wail, drawing the full to empty, draining them of hope."

The words played over and over in his mind. Were they merely the product of his dreaming mind, or were they something more unwholesome, something with weight? He took a sip of the acrid beer, trying to drown his own meloncholy in the liquid.

" . . . Ah, Josilfa and the Church will end them soon enough; they skirt around heresy too closely."

"What heresy? Don't they just yell about the Miseries?"

"Eh, no, they worship death itself. They think the dead will inherit the world, or some such."

That last bit snagged Dödz's attention. He didn't turn his head or eyes towards the conversation happening at the table behind him, but he listened closely.

"Now, I don't know exactly what they believe, but I heard they don't believe He and She are divine, so you know that's trouble." The first man's voice was wet and round sounding. He had a put-upon air of expertise that Dödz sincerely doubted he had earned.

"Wait, we're talking about the same people, right?" asked the second man. His scruffy voice was earnest; he believed that the first man was learned. Fool. "The guys in masks and robes who come about and arrange the dead?"

"Indeed, we are," the first answered.

"How do you mean they don't worship the Two? I saw a group of them just east of town earlier making some sort of . . . display. Looked to be a misery. I would guess that the Basilisks are all they worship."

"You would be wrong, is all I'm saying." The first sat back smugly.

"Where?" Dödz asked. His sudden appearance, standing beside their table, startled the two men.

"What?" asked the first, annoyed.

"Where were these cultists?" Dödz asked again.

"Oh, east of town, along the road that heads towards the Wasts." The second leaned forward and lowered his voice. "Is you with the Inquisition, then? Going to go and stop them from heresy they practice?" He sounded eager for juicy gossip.

But Dödz had already turned from the table and the two men, making his way out of the run down tavern, and turning towards the east.

Dödz Bringare was not a member of the Inquisition. He wasn't even a member of Josilfa's Church. It was his distinct belief that the gods were dead or had fled. Anything left in this horrid dying reality was not worth worshiping. The Basilisks were powerful, and Verhu's prophecies held as much water as anything else, but he would be damned if he believed the things were gods.

But if there was a cult, one who tapped into prophecies of miseries that did not coincide with Verhu's mutterings, then they might have some insight into his strange dreams. If they believed the world would be inherited by the dead, that would at worst make them allies of the Dead Saint Skelvik. At best, their theology would be opposed to Dödz.

Dödz was a hunter of ghuls, a slayer of the rotting damned. His bread and butter were putting to bed those things that rose from an unhallowed rest. He was decent at his chosen path, too; he had managed to end plenty of undead monsters without joining their ranks. Though close calls were getting closer and more deadly, seemingly by the day. Another side effect of being in the last days of a dying world.

He made his way east, winding through the small town. Everywhere around him, people were living their short miserable lives. One could be forgiven for assuming more of the miseries had come than had actually struck. Everywhere he looked was poverty and pestilence. Those who were in mourning—in colors only, too numbed by the brutality of the world to actually shed tears any longer—went about their day, peddling wares and doing small jobs to make ends meet. The end of the world didn't mean shit for most of them; nothing did.

Dödz was worse off; he had the most terrible of afflictions.

Hope. He knew it was a false hope, like fool's gold. Worthless but for the hunger and drive it instilled in him. He knew that, even if he were to find Skelvik and destroy the monstrous lich, it wouldn't stop the world from ending. It wouldn't stop anything other than one undead sorcerer's plans. But maybe it would help the world keep spinning for a few more days, hours, or minutes. Those minutes might be painful and terrifying, but they were all he had to count his life by, and he would fight for every single second of them.

He spotted the group of cultists easily. Unlike most death cults, they weren't hiding in the shadows. Dressed in black robes that covered them from head to toe and sporting metallic death masks, they worked in near silence. Taking corpses out of a nearby wagon, they set them into a tableau, tying the limbs with bits of twine to bent wire and wooden frames to crate a scene. Dödz's first suspicion was that the cultists *were* undead themselves. But watching them banished the thought. The dead moved with either the halted jerking motions of rigor-mortis, or an unnatural fluidity. These men and women moved with the fatigue and weariness that was the purview of the living.

He watched them work from a distance. He wasn't alone in doing so; many villagers were gathered about watching the morbid display. The cultists didn't seem to mind either; it was likely the entire point of this act was garner new followers.

As they worked, Dödz could make out the scene being constructed. A priest of some sort preaching to a choir of the dead, amongst them a man with teeth too big for his mouth wielding a massive sword, attacking a smaller man with nothing but a dagger in hand. Behind the priest, another corpse, a woman, stood head down, her ragged limp hair barely hiding the smile that one of the cultists had forced her face into.

Dödz's blood ran cold; he knew this scene. He had lived it. But how could these robed figures know about it? How could they rebuild that terrible fight with Numen? Dödz certainly hadn't told anyone, and Numen was fucking dead.

He took a step forward, ready to confront the cult, when the sound of a dismal horn cut through the air. The Inquisition of Josilfa had come, servants of the Two-Headed Basilisks, bullies and killers all. Three Inquisitors sat on horses. They were scarred men, brutes in the black armor of their cause: they smiled at the panic their presence birthed.

The townsfolk ran back towards their houses, wanting no part in what was to come. After all, it took very little for the Inquisition to decide you were involved with a heresy.

Dödz did not run. He watched, his hand near the handle of his hand-axe, waiting. The cultists didn't run either. Instead, they milled about, unsure of themselves, before one detached from the group and approached the three mounted Inquisitors.

They spoke for a few minutes, the man on horseback staring down, his face a grim line of zealous hate. The men that flanked him were not so stoic; they laughed at the conversation. It looked to Dödz as though they were egging each other on, mocking the cultist. The robed cultist, on the other hand, was growing more animated, more agitated, arms waving through the air as though trying to explain a point to an extremely slow toddler.

This continued for a few moments more, before the Inquisitor in front lifted his hand, revealing a small crossbow, and launched a bolt through the cultist's mask. The others watching screamed in horror as the three dismounted and started forward.

Dödz was presented with a choice: let the Inquisition kill of these cultists and seek his answers somewhere else, or step in, making himself an enemy of the Church, risk his life, and then see if the cultists knew anything that could help him find and put an end to Skelvik the Profane.

The latter seemed far and away the shittier of the choices. It would risk his life not only now, but for the foreseeable future, what little of it there was.

But then again, this was his first lead towards anything resembling an answer, and to see that lead wash away in blood as the fanatics were killed by a different, more aggressive group of fanatics was just too frustrating a thing to watch. He stepped forward, wondering if he should take the time to attempt to broker peace, maybe end all of this without bloodshed.

He continued having this thought as he plucked the hand-axe off his belt and threw it. He considered what he could say to give the Inquisitors pause in their bloody work as it tumbled end over end through the air. The sound of the weapon burying itself in the skull of the nearest Inquisitor brought his focus back to the here and now. Reality was always more bloody than ideal. The other two men hadn't noticed that their partner had been killed yet. This suited Dödz just fine as he ran to the twitching corpse of his victim and lifted the sword from his dead hands.

That movement caught the eye of the Inquisitor farthest from him, and he began to shout. The first man, the one with the crossbow, started to turn towards Dödz, but it was too late for him. Dödz hadn't stopped moving and he was already there, already swinging the sword. While the Inquisitors had just clocked his presence, he had been considering how to fight them from the moment he laid eyes on them. Instead of aiming for a vital organ, Dödz sliced through the visible gap in armor on the man's thigh. He cried out, and fell to his knee, surprised by the sudden explosion of pain. Without missing a beat, Dödz drew back and launched forward, driving the length of the blade through the man's neck.

Instead of pulling the sword free, Dödz dipped and grabbed the hilt of his fresh kill's short sword, and brought it up just in time to deflect the downward swing from the last Inquisitor standing. He would have preferred to kill all three before they could get their bearings, but this one was faster on the draw than expected. Dödz rose, deflecting two more strikes. On the third, he pushed hard, knocking the other man's blade away. He raised his foot to plant a kick square on the Inquisitor's chest, sending him sprawling backwards onto his ass.

"In for a copper . . . " Dödz muttered, walking forward. Perhaps his crime would be less severe if he didn't murder all three, but conversely, his crime wouldn't matter if none of them survived to report him.

"Back, you piece of shit; we serve the Church!" the fallen holy man spat at Dödz.

"Used to," Dödz corrected.

"What?"

"You used to serve the Church, and you used to be a *we*. Now you're just a *you*. And the dead serve no one, so, all of that is in the past. Your future, on the other hand . . . well, it serves the worms."

The man raised his sword, but Dödz kicked it away effortlessly before straddling him and slitting his throat. Messy work, but it was fine. He turned, expecting that the cultists had long since fled, but was surprised to see that they were still there. Not only had they not fled, they had come closer, grabbing and dragging the newly fashioned corpses towards their cart. One of them approached him.

“Herr Bringare?” His voice was soft, and muffled by the mask he wore.

“Hamfund?” Dödz asked, caught off guard to find the squire he had met in Lord Crol’s dungeon here.

“Ah, yes sir. Indeed.” The short fat man reached for his mask and then seemed to think better of it and left it on. “I . . . am surprised to see you sir.”

“Not half so much as I am to see you, Hamfund. I had heard that your fiefdom had been the center of . . . some . . . ” He trailed off.

“A misery, sir.” Hamfund supplied.

“Yes, that.” Dödz said, eying the metal mask that hid Hamfund’s face. It looked like a shattered mirror that had been glued together in the shape of a smiling visage. “How did you survive?”

“Well, sir, I was actually away from home when the misery occurred, visiting my mum in Grift. When I returned . . . ” He shrugged.

“So you joined a death cult?” Dödz asked.

“I didn’t realize it was a death cult at the time. They were aiding survivors and respectfully gathering the dead; it just seemed like a polite group helping out. One thing led to another and then . . . ” he gestured sort of ineffectually at the tableaux they had been building out of corpses.

Dödz looked at the scene they had constructed. It was straight from the nightmares he had been experiencing since that night in the Kergis church. “How do you build these . . . murals?”

“We’re given a diagram from the Priestesses,” Hamfund answered helpfully.

“And where are they?”

“They pretty much keep to themselves in Krunearils.” Hamfund spoke before clamping his hand over the mouth of his mask.

“The necropolis just inside the Valley?” Dödz clarified,

watching the mirrored death mask of the squire. Finally Hamfund nodded. "Then I suppose I'll need to pay them a visit. And Hamfund?"

"Sir?" The dejected squire-turned-cultist asked.

"Find different friends, Hamfund."

"Sir."

Dödz turned and walked away from the scene of the slaughter and the tableaux that had been half-built.

His suggestion had been given for a few reasons. Death cults only ever ended one way, in death. But with the bodies of three Church officials near the site of one of this cult's little displays, surely their death would come sooner rather than later. And depending on how chatty the cultists were when it happened, death would likely come for *him* shortly after. It wouldn't be his first time on the wrong side of the law, or the Church.

Worrying about that could come later; now it was time to steal a horse and make his way across the dying lands to Krunearils.

II

The dying lands.

It wasn't a name, not a proper one; it was a title the shared collective of this world had given itself. It spoke to a fatalism so brutal and unforgiving that hope was no longer even worth entertaining. Each person, no matter if they were born a begger or a king, knew that the end was coming. They, like the lands, would all die. Be it in a decade or be it tomorrow, the end had already been spoken into being and there was no escaping it.

But perhaps it could be delayed.

That was as much hope as Dödz could hold onto. He understood the hubris of such a statement, and more so, the hubris of assuming Skelvik the Profane, the dead saint who whispered in his dreams and screamed in his nightmares, was the key to postponing the end of all things. But, like his life, it was all that he had.

Days of hard riding brought him to the grave complex of Krunearils. It was as dismal as he remembered last he had passed by. It had been decades ago, his father having dragged him and his brothers on a hunting trip into the Valley of the Unfortunate Dead, a journey to teach his sons the family business of corpse-slaying.

A semi-successful venture. The boys had survived, but barely. The experience had driven Herschan to seek an escape from reality through narcotic alchemical injections; he was dead within the year. Arik became cruel, finding he had a penchant for violence and murder, and did not like to keep that constrained only to the undead. Dödz made it out, mind intact, but faith in any gods frayed to the point of breaking. Their mother never forgave their father for the way the trip had ripped apart her boys. Within a month, she had absconded with a chunk of the family fortunes and a lover who had no interest in fighting ghuls.

All of these bitter memories flooded into Dödz's mind as he sat upon the stolen horse, glaring at the complex of tombs and graves. Back then, it hadn't been swarming with black-robed and mirror-masked cultists. He dismounted, hitching the horse to a nearby dead tree. If the horse had it in mind to run, it could easily uproot the rotten thing, but Dödz was hopeful that the resistance provided by the anchor would keep the beast in place. He patted the horse's neck twice to reassure it before walking towards the mausoleum network.

Above him stretched a great arch carved into the likeness of two skeletal giants. As he grew closer, he could see that those giants were actually made of thousands of carved stone skeletons. The dead making up the dead. He hoped this was artistic license and there was no conglomerate bone-fiend waiting for him inside.

A voice suddenly called from within the shadows of the massive doorway. "Beware the coming of the dread dawn! The sun rises again, scorching the world clean of flesh!"

"Beware," echoed another voice. "The devouring worms rise from rain-soaked earth, thrashing! The waters below join the waters above and the writhing brings the end!"

"Beware, as hunter becomes hunted!" a third voice cried. "And they who carry the sacrilegious blood are gutted and bled dry to feed the coming apocalypse!"

Dödz approached, gripping the hilt of the sword he'd taken off the corpse of the Inquisitor. It was a fine weapon, silver coated, an ostentatious bullshit that would grant him a slight edge with certain monsters, though he had hoped he wouldn't have to put it to the test quite so soon. As he came closer he saw a massive man shaped-abomination, a towering undead covered in black funerary ash. In its hands it carried a basket, and it was from this basket that the cries and prophecies were being shouted.

Dödz frowned as the ash-blackened behemoth came closer. The basket contained a multitude of heads, each crying out some dire portent. The hulking brute stopped at the top of the steps, staring down at Dödz.

"Beware, Dödz Bringare, third of his name, last of his line, who washes away hope with mead and drowns his insecurity in the coagulated blood of the undying!"

"That is no prophecy; that is just a title," Dödz grumbled.

It was true he was the third man of his family to bear the name Dödz, and it was no surprise he would be the last; he was no romantic seeking to woo and breed. He stepped closer, wary of the towering undead.

Each of the heads in the basket was in a different stage of decay, though all of them moved. They flexed their cheeks and tongues, using what muscles existed in their rotting faces to turn towards Dödz.

"No prophecy? Have we not stated enough?"

"Have you not had your fill?"

"You know the miseries come in droves, not dribbles."

Dödz waved the warnings away, along with the flies

that rose from the basket. He spared a look at the giant corpse, but it was passive, seeming uncaring of his presence.

"Still, dire warnings that things are shit and will become shittier is hardly a prophecy; it's simply a statement of fact."

One of the heads used its tongue to reposition itself and stare up at him. Its eyes were dead, milky and worm-eaten. It raised an eyebrow, somehow managing to look snarky as a decapitated head.

"So judgmental, Bringare; you are not better than us," it chided.

"More mobile," Dödz returned.

"More *mobile*," the head mocked. "You come to our home, to our palace . . . why are you here, Bringare?"

"I thought you were a prophet; don't you know?"

"A prophet, he says!" exclaimed another head buried further in the basket. "Singular? Do we look attached? No, we are prophets, plural!"

"Prophets. Sorry; don't you all know, then?" Dödz corrected himself.

"Yes."

"Yes."

"Of course."

"Yeah, look," the head at the top of the pile said. "We don't get a ton of visitors. Other than the pilgrims, and they are horrible, just plain horrible at this; they come and act all worshipful. Nice at first, sure, but rubbish for interesting talking."

"I'm not here for conversation," Dödz said flatly.

"No, of course not. You're here to discover the truth, the reason for the miseries. The source of all prophecy."

"Close enough to true. Will you stop me? Will you try?"

"Stop you?" The heads began laughing. "No. Even if we could, why would we? If you are stupid enough to seek the truth, let that be the end of you. We are not the Basilisks' misguided Church; we will not deny you your own undoing."

"You're saying going inside is a death sentence." Dödz stated.

"For some. Perhaps not for you, with your sword and your grit and the hatred in your belly. But seeking the truth will unmake you as surely as any tool of death."

"I suppose I will just have to take my chances," Dödz said as he stepped around the hulking behemoth and its basket of loose heads. "Thanks for the warning, though."

It felt strange, not killing the monstrosity behind him. Letting the undead live, turning his back on them, were easy ways to die. But these didn't seem hostile. Maybe that was the new world, the new status quo. Maybe even the dead were just trying to exist until the end came to wipe everything out. He couldn't fight every evil in the world; there was just too much. He had to choose his battles, and a few lonely babbling heads seemed a small enough thing to let go.

Without a further look back, Dödz walked through the doors of the Necropolis, ready to face the terrible truth he had been warned about.

IIII

Fetid and dark. Always fetid and dark.

Just once, Dödz would love to walk into a beautiful marble temple with sprawling skylights. A place where you didn't have to squint in the torchlight just to make out what was in the corners. Somewhere where the smoke from the torches didn't fill your lungs and sting your eyes to the point even the well lit areas were obscured by your tears.

But, no, it was always fetid and dark, with the smell of rotting feet and ammonia-thick stench of vermin's leavings. This was the life he had chosen. And what a fucking choice it was. His brother had the right of it, drink and whore until they put you in the ground. Why bother with all this . . . what could loosely be called heroism? Where did it get you in the end?

Why, it got you exactly where Dödz was. A fetid and dark necropolis surrounded by the dead and those that worshiped them.

He pulled one of the guttering torches free of its fixture. Raising it high over his head, as much to get the smoke out of his eyes as to illuminate, he looked around. The antechamber was a wide semi-circle. Every few feet along the outer wall, doorways led into deeper, darker, probably even more fetid hallways and chambers.

But that was a secondary concern; Dödz quickly realized he wasn't alone. All around him were cots laden with corpses. A buffet of the dead laid out on a platter. Between the cots were masked and robed figures of cultists. They moved like scurrying ants attending to the eggs of their queen. Anointing bodies with oils, shooing off rats, writing in books, or in more cases, inscribing sigils on the cold dead forms at their feet. Dödz grabbed one of the attendants as they ran past.

"What?" The attendant squealed, startled and frightened. A woman, Dödz assumed by the tenor of her voice.

"What are you doing?" he growled at her.

"I'm . . . I'm taking care of the newly arrived, as the Holy Mother ordered!" She stammered, pulling weakly at her arm in an attempt to free herself.

"Newly arrived? Newly arrived from where?"

"Ah, Galgenbeck, these are the dead from Galgenbeck! Please . . . please let me go . . . "

Dödz released her with a sigh and turned his attention to the doorways. "Where do these lead?"

The masked woman tilted her head for a moment, rubbing her arm where he had grabbed her, as if certain he had broken the limb. Despite the mask, she looked as if trying to decide if he was insane. Strictly speaking, the necropolis wasn't off limits to those who were not cult members, but it was . . . odd to see someone else here.

Finally, she shrugged. "Deeper. They lead deeper.

What you find if you go deeper isn't up to us, but to the Wolkath himself. If you are worthy, he will show-—"

Dödz rolled his eyes and walked away. He had wanted information, not some bullshit scripture from the mouth of the newly indoctrinated. The worst part, in his opinion, was that her bullshit may not be bullshit. He had been alive long enough to see that the world operated on its own logic, and if there was some local god pulling the strings here, he could be fucked before he even got underway. But it wasn't worth worrying about. Instead, he chose a doorway at random and barged through, thrusting the torch out ahead of himself to guide the way.

The passage extended on and on, at a slight downward slant that gave the illusion of descending hundreds of miles below the earth. That didn't bother Dödz too much; he had gone underground before, explored catacombs. There had been a time when doing this sort of thing excited him. When he had wanted to be a hero, when he thought doing so would net him women and riches. When he had thought that not only could he save the world, but that the world was worth saving.

That had been a lifetime ago. He could feel the weight of the little prayer-book in his pocket, laden with all of those memories and regrets. Perhaps he could bury it down here with the gods-damned dead and the damned dead gods. Perhaps not, though: perhaps he would hold on to it, call on the last few vestiges of power it had to survive another day. What else was there, other than survival?

Ahead of him, the passageway evened out and doorways began appearing on either side. Dödz wished he had taken the time to research the necropolis, its actual layout, how far it extended. Good questions; any hunter of the dead worth their salt should know the answers. But Dödz was more salty than his worth, and refused to turn back.

Reaching the first door, he glanced in and saw a priestess, arms raised to the darkness. A group of pilgrims knelt before her in quiet repose. Dödz considered interrupting; he felt no sanctity or kindness towards a death cult, especially one who worshiped at the feet of Nechrubel's herald, Wolkath. As he watched, the priestess dipped a silver ritual knife into a basin of water and then brought the blade into contact with a small bowl of glowing coals. The hiss echoed through the chamber.

But the truth was, he wasn't here to fuck with the cult. He was here for answers. He passed the door and kept on his way.

So far, this was easy, which made him suspicious; death worshiping cults did not usually let people waltz into their strongholds and meddle in their affairs. By now, he would have expected to have been beset by madmen, attacked my the undead, mocked by wizards, threatened by monsters, and all other manner of unpleasantness. If he were able to just find the head priest or priestess and get some answers, then get out without bloodying himself or his blade, he would have to consider it the most success he had ever had.

Dödz rounded a bend in the hallway and came up short. Before him, huddled in the dust and dirt, were several rotting figures hunched over the corpse of a cultist, eagerly shoving fistfuls of quivering meat into their mouths. Dödz stood silent for a second, the sputtering light of his torch washing over the gruesome scene. It wasn't surprising; you lock yourself in a necropolis you're bound to lose a few to being eaten.

IV

Dödz stepped forward, drawing his blade and slashing in one movement, catching the nearest ghul on the chin.

The blade shattered. Dödz fell back and drew his dirk

from its home in his boot, angling his body to keep the torch between himself and the creatures. He had never lost a blade to a ghul's head before. Now that he was taking a moment, he could see that parts of them were not rotting flesh, but rusted iron, as though someone had bolted iron prosthetics to decaying bodies.

The only thing worse than the unquiet dead, were the unquiet dead that were brought about by human hands. Dödz looked them over, keeping the ghuls at bay with the torch as he figured out how to dispatch them. In the end, these things would die (again) as any armored opponent did. He moved quickly, jamming the torch into the midsection of the one on the right. Dried flesh and ragged clothes caught quickly, the sticky pitch clinging and turning it into a pyre.

As the ghul squealed and flailed in feral fear, Dödz turned and slashed with the dirk, aiming under the armored ribs of the next. Papery flesh tore easily, but no guts spilled out. Dödz reversed his grip and brought the knife back and up, digging inches of steel into the chest cavity. The creature didn't seem to mind pushing itself down onto the blade, teeth snapping a breath's width from his face.

"Fuck you," Dödz growled. He pushed with his legs to force them both to jump, then thrust hard with the dirk as they came back down, the momentum forcing the ghulto be impaled further. The blade ripped through desiccated organs and emerged from its mouth, breaking teeth as it did.

Dödz kicked it off his blade, watching just long enough to make sure the light was fading from it eyesockets. He was about to turn back to the still-burning ghul when the third, unharmed, tackled him. His dirk went skittering across the floor as dirty claws raked his face, drawing bloody grooves in the skin. He wedged an arm between himself and the ghul, trying to push it off, or at least keep it from getting closer. Bracing his elbow against its sternum, he quested with his other hand for anything he could use as a weapon.

"I'm not fucking dying in a crypt." Dödz grunted, squinting through the blood flowing into his eyes from the scratches.

He worried that his words were hollow. That, despite his intentions, despite his grit and willpower, this was how he would face his end: buried under the snapping jaws of an iron clad ghul. He writhed, trying to get free, trying to get his legs up so he could kick. But it gave no quarter. Dödz was getting tired, his muscles ached with a burn that told him he wouldn't be able to hold out much longer.

"Ah, you must be the visitor." A voice, creased with age whispered just above the sound of the rasping undead.

Dödz didn't dare look away, the ghul intent on tearing out his throat. He considered ignoring the voice, but decided against that.

"Why are you here, visitor?" The voice questioned.

"Your prophecies concern me," Dödz said. "The display you lot were putting up, in Postek. I knew the scene. It was nearly the death of me."

The voice didn't respond for a long time, and Dödz didn't have the luxury of turning to see if anyone was even there. After more moments of tense struggle, Dödz saw a pair of boots in his periphery vision. Boots, and a dagger, held by a black gloved hand. The dagger slammed through the side of the ghul's skull. It snapped its teeth twice more, then all animation fled and itcollapsed, freeing Dödz.

Dödz finally turned to look at his savior. The figure was clad in black robes and a metal funerary mask. Male, he would guess, from the larger frame and shape of their shoulders under the cloth material. The knife was in one hand, up and ready to strike like a scorpion's tail. The other hand was offered to Dödz.

He took it, using his counterbalance to push himself upright.

"Thank you."

The figure did not answer, retreating to an entourage of cultists. Their robes were lined in silver thread, and they appeared stooped with age.

"You are welcome," his savior said. "I would ask what you meant by what you said, but now I recognize you. I know you from visions whispered by Wolkath, in my dreams. You are the hunter who stalks the crypts and seeks to keep the dead quiet."

"Close enough; my name is—"

"Neither I, nor anyone else present here today, cares what your name is," cut in another, a woman by the sound of her voice. "You come seeking answers; what makes you think we have any?"

"You spout prophecies that differ from those of Verhu," Dödz answered. There was a gasp at his blase and casual use of the Basilisk's name. He ignored it and continued. "So did the lich, Skelvik, when I confronted him, a confrontation that was being recreated using corpses in Postek. Which leads me to make some assumptions."

"You know what they say about when you assume," the woman said, sounding more like a grandmother than anything else.

"Am I wrong?" Dödz pressed.

"That depends on the assumptions. If you assume we know more about your fate, or this Skelvik, then yes. You are wrong. If your assumption is that we access prophecies hidden even from HE and SHE, well, then you would be right, but again it depends on what you assume, what you seek, what you crave."

"The truth, and a way to stop Skelvik. To stop the dead from inheriting the earth." Dödz bent over to pick up his dirk.

There was no telling how these fanatics would react to his remarks. They were a death cult, and death cults dealt in death. Death to themselves, death to others; it was a toss up of which this would be.

"We cannot help you there," she said. "The dead *will*

inherit the world; there is no stopping that. But you mean you wish to stop Skelvik from raising an undead army that will destroy this world even faster. You wish to stop his prophecies from coming true before HIS do."

"What is the difference? I don't care if the undead serve Selvik or themselves; I don't want—"

"We don't mean the living dead. Or, maybe we do." The priestess shrugged. "No matter what you do, you won't stop what is coming, but we will not stop you from trying. You wish to see, to know what to do next, maybe we can help." She paused for a moment and then nodded. "Yes, I think we can." She moved to her right and opened a door that Dödz had missed before. "Enter, and be enlightened."

Dödz didn't trust the priestess any more than any other cultist. But, if they had wanted him dead, all they would have had to do was wait for the ghul to tear out his throat. He watched them warily as he approached; the cultists for their part gave him a wide berth, taking a step back for every step he took forward.

When he reached the door, he peered into the darkness beyond. He couldn't make anything out. He retrieved the sputtering torch he had used to kill the first ghul and held it aloft before him, and caught his breath.

V

Stone walls stretched out of sight, the ceiling lost in shadows, soaring impossibly tall.

Every surface was adorned with carved figures being tortured, reliefs so rife with lurid detail of abuse as to make it seem the stone itself writhed in agony. In the center of the room, a small ridge was raised from the floor, the rim of some well, or pool. Its stagnant water filled the air with a thick, mildewy stench.

Dödz glanced back and saw that the cultists had vacated the doorway, either waiting out of sight or having moved on with whatever they'd been doing when they came across him. As he approached the well, he noticed that the carved figures were not only on the walls . . . their leering, pain-filled faces covered the floor as well. The entire room was a testament to cruelty and agony.

Unwilling to give into the unnatural fear that filled his gut like ice, he knelt at the rim, staring into the dark depths. All he saw was murky water choked with mold and slime, flitting insects, and larvae.

This was a fool's errand; there was nothing for him to find, nothing for him to achieve here. He started to rise when his own reflection, distorted and rotting, exploded from the water. It seized him by the neck and pulled him in. The water was tepid, cool as a long dead corpse. He could feel the aquatic larvae writhing against his flesh, parasites seeking entry through pores and orifices. Dödz struggled, trying to break free of his double's clammy grip, but no matter how hard he fought, he was trapped.

His lungs burned. His muscles ached. He couldn't hold his breath any longer, couldn't keep fighting it.

He opened his mouth for a final cry of defiance.

And inhaled air, not stagnant water.

He breathed deep, shocked by the sudden realization that he could breathe at all. In fact, other than a weird sense of weightlessness, he didn't feel like he was submerged, or that his grim duplicate had him by the throat anymore.

Opening his eyes, he found himself somehow floating above a bubbling swamp in the midst of a terrible storm. Twisted mangrove trees writhed in the wind, the hellish landscape illuminated in flashes of evil-looking green lightning.

Then, he saw himself, or yet another version of himself, lantern shield at the ready, facing down another familiar figure. None other than Skelvik the Profane, the dead saint, bishop of the rotting congregation, hurling bolts of necrotic energy.

Dödz could do nothing but watch the two figures wage a bitter war in the swamp. His other double expertly wove in and out of reach of Skelvik's spells, but was unable to close the distance to attack the lich.

The swamp's waters churned with the undead damned, surfacing to join Skelvik's assault. Dödz saw himself overwhelmed by the surging dead, as Skelvik approached, ready to destroy him.

Suddenly, behind Skelvik, roaring through the gloom, two reptilian heads rose into view, monstrous in size and bearing draconic visages replete with antlers. Unholy sigils whirled in the air around them. He did not know if they were HE or SHE, but THEY looked not at the war being fought, but straight at the weightless Dödz floating above the battlefield.

Believe, or not. The end comes. The heathens and blasphemers, the zealots and faithful. All fall. All die. All rot away to nothing. Skelvik seeks to undo OUR word. He seeks to become Nechrubel's foil and usurp the true way of things.

The words tolled in Dödz's brain with such power he thought he felt blood dripping from his ears.

"And what of it?" he shouted, straining to be heard above the din of the storm and his own agonizing death taking place below—Skelvik reaching into the other Dödz's mouth, stretching his jawto plunge shoulder deep and rip out vital organs. "What is my path?"

One of the heads of THEY moved close enough for Dödz to sense its rancid breath .

You do as you do. Your path comes for you. None may waylay OUR will.

Next he knew, the world was spinning away from him in a dizzying kaleidescope of colors, as if he'd been violently flung an unfathomable distance. Then he was sputtering and coughing on his hands and knees, head throbbing, beside the well he had been dragged into.

Or not; he was dry as a bone. It had all been a vision.

Dödz attempted to rise, but fell back down, unable to catch his balance just yet.

From outside the room, he heard shouting, and the clash of blades. It sounded like the Inquisition had caught up with the cultists . . . and with him. Dödzmade sure both the torch and his blade were near at hand. He may not have had a fighting chance, but, gods-damnit he wouldn't go down without trying.

He rose, taking a moment to get his bearings before heading towards the door.

As he reached the doorway, an armoured figure appeared, pointing its sword at Dödz. He parried with his dirk. His opponent was quick, and well trained, letting his sword fall away, offering no resistance and throwing Dödz off balance once more . . . only to drive a heavy punch into Dödz's gut. The blow sent him sprawling to the floor. Dödz got ready for the execution, intent on meeting his end as a man.

"Hello, Dödz."

The voice from beneath the helmet was familiar, but it had been so long since he had heard that voice, he could barely believe it was possible.

"No . . . there's no way," Dödz muttered, pulling himself to his feet. He still held the dirk, but it seemed silly now. "No."

"Hardly a fine way to greet your brother."

VI

"Arik?" His brother, here? And in a military uniform too? It seemed entirely ridiculous. Who would enlist Arik? Who would make him an officer? Dödz wondered if someone had purposefully sent him. Who better to kill a Bringare than another Bringare? "Here to put the nails in my coffin for Josifa?"

"I'm not with the Inquisition. Finding you is a happy

coincidence. I wasn't looking for you. I mean . . . " He paused considering his words. "I have been looking for you, but that's not why I am here."

"Then why are you here?" Dödz asked.

Arik removed his helmet. It was almost like looking into a mirror, except instead of the rough and disheveled face that Dödz knew he presented, Arik was well kept and sported a luxurious mustache. He was older, but had only a fraction of the pained aging Dödz knew lined his own face. "It matters not. What does matter is that you are officially conscripted."

"What?" Dödz asked, dumbfounded.

"Time to fulfill your glorious purpose, brother. With the miseries unleashed upon the world, it's finally time to do something about it. To strike back against the evil festering in the Valley of the Unfortunate Dead. Welcome to the Boneheart Crusade, Dödz."

THE SILVERED BAGLIN (ADVENTURE)

BRIDGET D. BRAVE

- **River/cavern** adventure
- **Setting**—On a river in the Wasts
- **Premise**—Steal treasure from demented witches for great reward!
- ***Meant for classless Scvm***

"Don't wander up the Quagpyre. There is something festering, something clotted, something rotten nestled deep in the moist crevasse of the river's mouth."

The Beggar's Inn

Rain slakes over the dirty tiled roof, running off in grey rivulets that further dim the yellowed glass. There's no sense in walking out into that deluge of runoff bathwater. Not that the inside is much cleaner: floors that haven't seen a mop in a fortnight, the filthy stickiness of drink and vomit clinging to the corners of the room, the heady scent of burning sagebrush mixing with the foul stench rather than covering it.

Not the fanciest of accommodations, but acceptable to

seek respite from the storm. You are offered stale bread. and a mug with spittle noticeably floating on the surface of the pisswarm beer. While warming your freezing bones at the meager fire, your eyes are drawn to a sheet of parchment. The page is suspiciously clean, the weave of the fibre expensive and otherworldly. Pinned with a jeweled clasp to the wall, it announces a "Reward for Intrepid Adventurers."

The First Duke of Cragthorn, the appointed Guardian of the Wasts and Master of the Underbrewery, seeks the able-bodied and stout of heart to recover his most holy stolen treasure, a Work of Arte and Relick known as the Silvered Baglin, from the Quagpyre Witches. Must possess the ability to swim. Magic resistance a plus. Payment upon delivery, 300 crowns.

The others in the inn shift away as you scrutinize the sheet, muttering into their mugs and making a hand gesture common among the rural folk. You recognize this as a ward against evil.

These folk will likely know the location of the Quagpyre Witches, but will likely need coaxing to give up their knowledge.

The River's Bend

Reached by road from the Inn, this "river" is more a trickle of something rust-colored, too thick and coagulated to classify as "fluid." The smell of old blood and sweat, low tide and rotten meat waft from the north.

There's a copse of trees and overgrown bushes that might be concealing something boatlike to the west. The river bends to the east toward a burned village. The mouth of the river can be found to the north.

Winged Ship (d6 presence check, bushes): A small vessel that has no identifiable method of propulsion, as the wings do not appear to serve any function beyond decorative. Perhaps once painted white or light blue, now faded to a dingy brown that matches the surrounding environs. When placed in the river, it moves by absorbing any fluid in the area toward its source.

Corpse (d6 presence check, east route, downriver): This is a burned corpse that likely fled from the village. He has a charred letter in his hand that mentions a boon the witches can grant to anyone who assists with their dark ritual.

The River

Growing in both size and depth, the thick bloodlike water pulls you ever northward toward your destination. The trees become more encroaching as you travel north, until they have formed a tunnel that leads to the river source.

1D6 River Encounters:

- Rouge Wave: A sudden wave of blood overwhelms your ship, sinking it.
- Cupper. A mushroom-shaped fish that is deadly to the touch. HP 4. Necrotizing Pores: coming into contact with the flesh of the fish will drain 1 hp of rot damage until the affected area is treated or removed.

- Overwhelming Hunger: You are overcome with a hunger that eats at you.—1 morale for two rounds.
- The Minstrel: All players roll a D6. A 1 receives the overwhelming urge to compose and perform an original song about the river.
- Clotter: A friendly lump of clotted *something* near the shore offers you a boon. Choose +1 to Agility, Presence, Strength, or Toughness.
- Warm winds: A waft of warm air speeds the flow of the river, speeding you along your journey.
- GM note: The river portion can take as many turns as necessary to accommodate party size and allotted gametime.

Runza Cave

Deep in this cavern, a fissure in the rock releases a gush of crimson fluid. This is the home of the Crones of the Quagpyre. The Crones stay in the shadows while they speak with you in one, singular voice. They know why you are here and make you an offer: you can choose to try and take their prize, you can walk away, or you can assist in their ritual and receive a boon.

When revealed, the Crones are withered husks of their former selves, naked and cloaked only in the greasy overgrown hair, which clings to their figures and gives glimpses of the ruined flesh beneath.

If you choose to fight:

- Rote Tante (Crone): HP 15, Morale 20, Attack d6 rusty dagger, d4 special
- Rote Welle (Crone): HP 15, Morale 5, Attack d6 claws, d4 special.
- Rote Woche (Crone): HP 10, Morale 26, Attack d6 teeth, d4 special.

1d4 Crone Special Attacks

1) *What is that smell?* You vomit for one turn, unable to do anything else.
2) *Exhaustion* You sleep for 1d4 rounds
3) *What did you say?* You are overcome with rage at one of your fellow adventurers and can only attack them for one round.
4) *Uncontrollable sobbing* You are unable to stop crying for 1d4 rounds.—1 to toughness until you're able to pull yourself back together.

Weefsels

(d4 for #): HP 5, Morale 2, Attack D6 claws.

Weefsels are small, wrapped cotton dolls animated by the Crones, by dipping their heads into the rivers' waters.

Kelks

(d4 for #): HP 4, Morale—, Attack d6 bludgeoning

Kelks are stitched together with the parts of previous adventurers to form four-legged creatures slightly bigger than a housecat. They bludgeon with their thick limbs.

- If you choose to leave: Each player must roll a Toughness check to see if the Kelks and Weefsels attack.
- If you choose to assist: Players must decide who in their party to sacrifice. Remaining players can choose a boon from one of the Crones.

Boons:

- The all-seeing eye—Rote Tante will pluck out one of her eyes and offer it to you. This eye allows you to see inside crates, barrels, caskets, and other enclosed spaces. Unfortunately, it only works once embedded in the center of your forehead. Eye weeps uncontrollably.
- Scent of the ages—Rote Welle produces a bottle from somewhere (you are unable to see any pockets). Once

drunk, you can smell food, potions, poison, explosives, and gold. You also experience nausea for three turns after use.

- Elixir of heaven—Rote Woche provides you with a vial of a rheumy-looking fluid. Drinking this will cure all effects and restore HP.

The Silvered Baglin:
This . . . this is just half a bloated corpse dipped in silver paint. Whatever the Crones were hoping to resurrect from this, you cannot imagine. What the Duke wants with it, stranger still.

ICHORTHORN (ADVENTURE)

KEVIN WELCH

- **Forest/hovel/cavern** adventure
- **Setting**—In a village on the outskirts of Sarkash.
- **Premise**—Children have been abducted from the village in the night.
- ***Meant for classless Scvm***

THE CHILDREN OF ICHORTHORN HAVE BEEN ABDUCTED!

The small logging village of Ichorthorn lies on the outskirts of Sarkash, led by the cruel and overbearing village leader Urm Skogsavverkning. For generations, townsfolk of Ichorthorn have been logging and milling Sarkash and exporting the wares to whoever will pay.

One tragic morning, as the townsfolk awoke, they discovered all of the children of town had been snatched from their beds in the middle of the night, including Urm's only son, the rotund and privileged Daeru. Beastly tracks and drag marks, found outside the windows of the families, lead into the darkest, most primordial groves of Sarkash, where even the bravest loggers dare not tread.

Urm says he will pay anything to get his son back!

What have the locals heard? (d8 Rumors)

1) Hunters and trappers have seen some strange creatures lurking in the forest . . . (true)
2) A traveler says the neighboring village of Aurillac had something similar happen not more than one week ago . . . (true)
3) The forest spirits are angered by the logging and will take their revenge . . . (partially true)
4) The wails of a terrible beast can be heard for miles around . . . (true)
5) Groland the Sickly, the leader from the neighboring village, had the children abducted to take control of Ichorthorn . . . (false)
6) The children conspired for weeks to leave the village and serve The Blood Maiden of Sanalassio . . . (false)
7) The Arch-Rogue of Schleswig paid a pretty penny to acquire as many children as he could to bolster his ranks and overthrow King Fathmu IX . . . (false)
8) The children haven't been abducted; they are playing the most elaborate game of "hide & seek" . . . (false)

TRAVEL INTO THE FOREST OF SARKASH

Before the party ventures into Sarkash, Urm provides them a full water skin and d3 days dried food each, and just one of the following (roll a d4):
1) Firesteel
2)Oil lamp (pre + 6 hours of oil)
3)Medicine Box (stops bleeding/infection and +d6 hp, pre + 4 uses)
4)"Don't you think the food/water is enough?"

(GM NOTE)
When the party decides to head into the forest, have the player with the lowest Presence roll a d3+1 for how many days they travel.

Every morning, along with the Travel Checklist found in Feretory (optional), have the player with the highest Presence test DR12 to stay on course and keep following the tracks. If the roll fails, add another day of travel.

The forest of Sarkash is dense, root ridden, and difficult to traverse.

Roll for encounters every day of travel:
Day 1: roll d4 on the Animal Column of the Sarkash encounter table and d12 on the Appearance Column.
(*These creatures will be more of a* ***hindrance****, not aggressive to the party.*)
Day 2: roll d8 on the Animal Column of the Sarkash encounter table, and d12 on both Mutation (once) and Appearance Column (twice).
(*These creatures will be more* ***territorial****. Won't attack first, but will attack if provoked.*)
Day 3 (and beyond): roll d12 on the Animal, Mutation (twice), and Appearance Column (twice).
(*These creatures will be more* ***aggressive*** *and will attack first, despite initiative roll.*)
(GM note: after every encounter, have players make presence test, DR12 to find fragments of clothing/possessions of children)

D12 SARKASH ENCOUNTER TABLE

ANIMAL	MUTATION (roll 2xs)	APPEARANCE (roll 2xs)
d4 rabbits (hp 2, no armor, morale—, d2 claw)	Extra eyes on stalks:Can't be snuck up on, wins initiative.	Glowing
d4 squirrels (hp 2, no armor, morale—, d2 bite)	Pincers:D4 dmg, 1-8 chance to break limb	Matted/scabbed skin
d3 foxes (hp 3, no armor, morale 5, d4 claw/bite)	Scorpion Tail:D4 dmg, 2-6 chance of infection	Emaciated
d6 toads (hp 1, no armor, morale—)	Acidic discharge:d4 dmg for d4 rounds or until cleaned.	Oil slicked coat
d3 dogs (hp 4, no armor, morale 6, d4 claw/bite)	Poisonous warts:d4 dmg if ingested, can be collected for poison.	Open, festering wounds
d8 rats (hp 1, no armor, morale—, d2 bite)	Extra limbs:Grapple player for d4 rounds unless DR12 Str test to break free.	Stitched flesh
d4 badgers hp 5,—d2 armor, morale 6, d4 claw/bite)	Razor sharp quills:d4 dmg (dagger)	Too many sharp teeth
d3 owls (hp 3, flying dr14 to hit, morale 8, d4 beak/talon)	Hard plated skin:Add one armor tier	Enlarged throat sack
d2 bears (hp 12,—dr2 hide, morale—, d6 bite/d8 claw)	Clubbed tail:d6 dmg (mace)	Malformed antlers
d4 deer (hp 6,—d2 hide, morale 6, d6 antler/hoof)	Concussive shriek:DR12 Pre test or disoriented for d4 rounds	Webbed feet
d4 eagles (hp 5, flying dr14 to hit, morale 6, d6 beak/talon)	Toxic spray:d6 dmg, degrades armor 1 tier in d4 rounds if not cleaned.	Transparent flesh
d6 wolves (hp 5,—d2 hide, morale 10, d6 bite/claw)	Proboscis:d6 dmg, DR12 Tou test or d6 eggs injected in the player, hatching in d4 days.	Obscenely rotund

Upon completing the last day of following the drag marks, the party comes upon a small clearing with a dilapidated structure barely noticeable beyond the overgrown brush. A faint glow can be seen in the broken window, and the distant smell of a smoldering fire can be detected.

ICHORTHORN

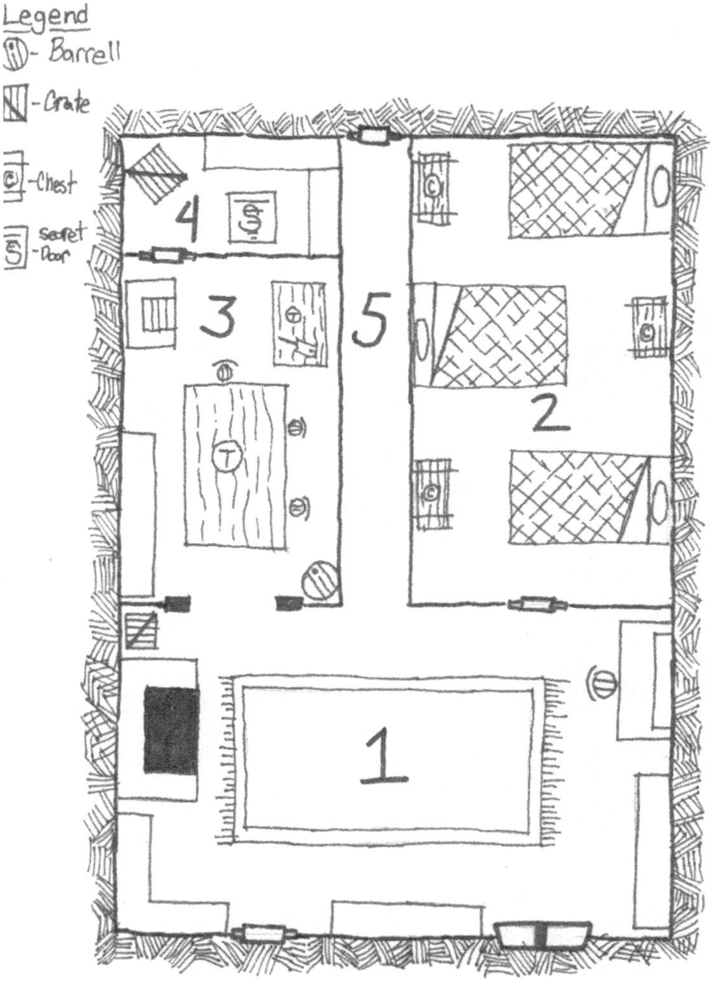

ROOM 1: FOYER

Stale air, smells of rotting foliage and mold. Scattered debris throughout.

North: Two doorways (N.E. and N.W) with a hallway between.

East: A desk, barely holding its form (Presence DR12 . On a success, roll on the d66 Corpse Plundering Table (Core Book). Also, a shelf with weather worn books, written in a long dead language.

South: Wooden door leading back to the forest with shelving on either side. More weatherworn books.

West: A fireplace, still warm from a neglected fire, and another shelf. More decaying books.

ROOM 2: BEDROOM

Locked door, Agility DR12 to unlock with lockpicks or Strength DR12 to break the door down, making quite the ruckus . . .

Musty and humid, smells of body odor and excrement.

North: Three unmade beds and three locked chests staggered in the room.

(GM note: first 2 chests are traps, Agility DR12 or take d4 dmg from spring loaded spikes in chests;, third one has the key to the padlock on the trap door in the Dry Storage room)

South: Door to Foyer

ROOM 3: KITCHEN

Uncomfortably warm, the stench of stale blood and rotten vegetables fills the air.

North: A long table, covered in refuse, in the center of the room with a door beyond it.

East: A butcher block table with a cleaver stabbed in it (d6 dmg) in the N.E. corner, a barrel in the S.E. corner, and a bone dry wash basin between.

Contents of the barrel (d4):
1) Pickled rats
2) Fermented entrails (DR12 toughness test or be infected)
3) D4 squirrels (roll from d12 Sarkash encounter table, once from each column)
4) Stagnant fetid water

South: Door to Foyer

West: Long bare shelves and a white-hot stove.

ROOM 4: DRY STORAGE

Dry, yet drafty

Empty shelves line each wall of this room, with crates haphazardly placed throughout.

(GM note: one player tests Presence DR12 to find a locked trap door under the crates. Key is found in the third chest in ***Bedroom.***)

Opening the trap door reveals an old wooden ladder descending into a basement, and the sound of distant screaming.

ROOM 5: HALLWAY

Dark and cobwebbed, a faint panting at the end of the hall.

A metal bowl at the entrance of the hall with the word "Behemoth" etched into it. Walking down the hall awakens a single dog, chained to the locked door behind it. The chain runs the length of the hall, and then some . . .

(GM note: roll on d12 Sarkash encounter table for dog's characteristics, twice on Mutations and Appearance)

KEVIN WELCH

THROUGH THE TRAPDOOR IN THE DRY STORAGE

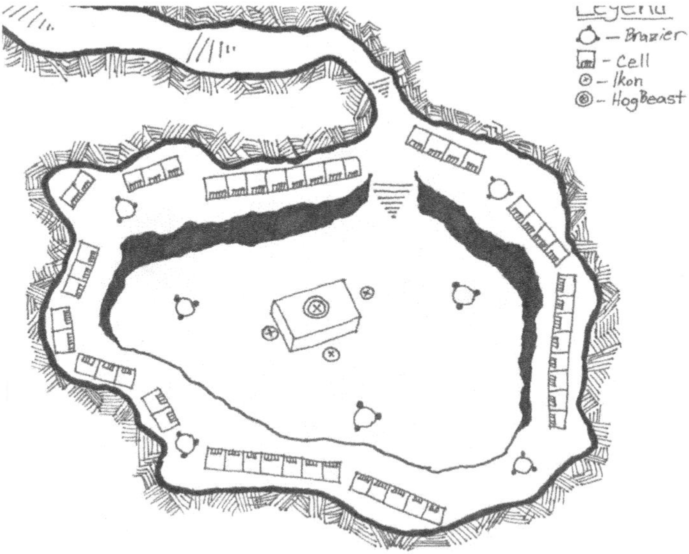

At the base of the ladder, there is a long hallway, crudely dug from the earth. An echoing melody of anguished screams and droning chants fill the hallway. At the end of the hallway is an enormous, cage-lined and braiser-lit room, with a hulking figure strapped to an altar and three ancient figures chanting around it.

The cages are filled with the children of the village, screaming in agony and half mutated, much like the animals the party encountered on the trail here. Test Agility DR12 or be noticed by the ancient figures. If noticed, roll Reaction. With a 9+, the ancient figures plead with the party and beg to let them finish what they started. Anything less on the Reaction roll causes them to release the Hulking HogBeast from the altar and send him charging towards the party.

THE IKONS OF SARKASH COMPLEX BACKSTORY

Generations ago, these three ancient figures were known as Börda, Agneth, and Kathan, sisters who warned the village of the calamity that would befall them if they kept logging the forests of Sarkash. Having heard enough of their protests, village leader and namesake Prestera Ichorthorn banished them to the very forest they warned the village about. Wandering lost and on the brink of death, the three bargained with the forest to spare them in exchange for their undying loyalty.

The spirits of the forest agreed, on one condition: for the three to devise a plan to rid the forest of the town that constantly threatens its life. Complying with the wishes of the forest, the three sisters abducted children who lost their way into the forest and transformed them into hideous beasts. With their ranks of bestial soldiers growing by the year, the three sisters had a strong enough force to raid the village in the night and abduct more offspring, transforming them, and planning to send them back to rain hell on Ichorthorn.

The sisters also reveal that the Hulking HogBeast is the son of Urm Skogsavverkning, Daeru, who willingly volunteered to be transformed, to spite his own father.

The Ikons of Sarkash

Hp—3 Morale—Armor—tattered robes (no armor) Weapon—none

Roll 2 Scrolls (One Clean, One Unclean) for each Sister. They cast one scroll per turn, each reading a scroll at the same time.

HogBeast (Daeru):

Hp—14 Morale—Armor—Thick bristled hide,—d4 Weapon—Glaive d8 dmg, Tusks d4 dmg

Special Attack—Charging Tusks, one player at random tests Agility, DR14 or takes d8 charging dmg and d4 tusk dmg. If Charging Tusks misses, HogBeast takes one turn to select another target for Charging Tusks.

The HogBeast protects The Ikons at all costs.

POSSIBLE OUTCOMES . . . (GM notes)

1) Kill the Sisters and possibly break the curse, turning the beasts (alive and dead) back to children, but still possessing the mutations.
2) The Sisters plead their case, convincing the party to take over the town in exchange for releasing the kids from the curse after the siege of Ichorthorn . . . maybe . . .
3) Imprison The Sisters and bring them to justice . . . as the town sees fit . . .
4) Party walks away, Urm thinks the party is involved with the abductions and places a bounty on their heads.

ABOUT THE CONTRIBUTORS

Charles R. Bernard is a writer who lives in Salt Lake City. He is the author of *A Baptism for the Dead* and *He Led Us Into the Wilderness and Spoke to Us*, among other novels. His short fiction has been featured in *Cosmic Horror Monthly, Deadman Humour: 13 Fears of a Clown*, and other publications and anthologies. He lives next to the largest city-operated cemetery in the United States, a sprawling necropolis that stretches over a square kilometer of grounds. He's lively enough company, though.

Harlen Linke is not a writer, but when asked to do so, what's one more creative hobby to stack onto the pile? He is probably best known for his level design endeavors for the video game *Team Fortress 2* under the nickname UEAKCrash, that often pushes the limits of the game and has seen official inclusion within it. Alternatively, maybe he's even better known for drumming, singing, producing, and engineering his doom metal band Bog Wizard, which embraces the era of satanic panic with tongue in cheek TTRPG/ fantasy elements, while still pointing a mirror on current societal injustices. Lesser chance, he might be known for his small laser engraving business Altfitters, which focuses on gaming products, art, and other custom merchandise. Even better, maybe he's just known as a dad of a 7-year-old feral goblin, and husband to an accomplished preschool teacher in a small Northern Michigan town.

Zac Goins is a balding grimlock who designs games and manages projects in the RPG space. He has written for dozens of publications, including entries in *D&D 5e, Marvel Multiverse, Mork Borg, Mothership, OSE, Pirate Borg, Vast Grimm* and more. He works for the publisher Limithron, creators of Pirate Borg. He lives near Kansas City, Kansas with his wife Megan and his two kids.

Ian SerVaas is a seasoned TTRPG editor and writer of over 50 different game products, and he also serves as the GM of the liveplay podcast Wandering Monster. When not shackled to his desk, you can find him running outside with a pack of feral raccoons. Ian lives in Indianapolis, Indiana, with his loving wife and two cats, Snacks and Rambo.

Zack Allen is a 90's kid raised on 80's pop culture, a lifelong fan of horror media, and an intrepid psychonaut. He spends most days battling against the weight of his own creative pursuits, but can also often be found kayaking the lake with his wife and dog, Siriusly, or watching too many cartoons. Please be kind, rewind.

John Baltisberger is an award-winning author, game designer, and the owner of Madness Heart Press. Through his writing, he has explored themes of mysticism, faith, sin, and personal responsibility. Known for his bizarre blend of Jewish mysticism and splatterpunk, his work has spanned extreme horror, urban fantasy, science fiction, cosmic horror, epic verse, and non-fiction. He lives in Austin, TX with his wife and his daughter.
linktr.ee/kaijupoet

Bridget D. Brave is an author and reluctant lawyer who is really lousy at writing bios. She can be found nearly everywhere online under beedeebrave.

Kevin Welch is a Northern California transplant, now living in Southern Colorado with his wife, 2 cats (Vyvyan and Bagheera), and dog Boris. When Kevin isn't working on projects for Madness Heart Games, he is a cast member and editor of the Flail to the Face, A "Compatible With Mörk Borg" Actual Play Podcast and cast member Wandering Monster, America's Test Table.

www.ingramcontent.com/pod-product-compliance
Ingram Content Group UK Ltd.
Pitfield, Milton Keynes, MK11 3LW, UK
UKHW041931101125
8878UKWH00001B/13

9 781955 745703